# Swords in the Summer

Mark Bartholomew

For
Fern and Hickory...
my friends in the trees!

## With great thanks to:

Crome Internet, Charlotte Keeley for jousting girls, Claire Whittenbury for coins in vinegar, Nicky and John Williams, Sarah Holmes for her Breton songs and dances, Tony Faughnan for his ideas and historical insights, Phillip Dawes at Waterstones, Lucy Butcher and especially to Alex for her unending support!

First published
September 07 in Great Britain by

PUBLISHING

© **Mark Bartholomew**

ISBN-10 1-905637-31-4
ISBN-13 978-1-905637-31-7

Educational Printing Services Limited
Albion Mill, Water Street, Great Harwood, Blackburn BB6 7QR
Telephone: (01254) 882080          Fax: (01254) 882010
E-mail: enquiries@eprint.co.uk          Website: www.eprint.co.uk

It has been almost a year since Fern and Hickory were discovered lost in the woods near the village of Woolpit. Since then, they and their friend, Nathaniel, have searched in vain for the children's father.

Their travels have taken them to the wild Suffolk coast, to the plague-ridden city of Lincoln, to the depths of Sherwood Forest and through the tunnels of Nottingham Castle.

Now, the three adventurers are heading to Cornwall where they hope to find the legendary Green Knight. Could he be the children's father? Will their journey end at last?

# Contents

Part Two - The Holly Crown

# Medieval Cornwall

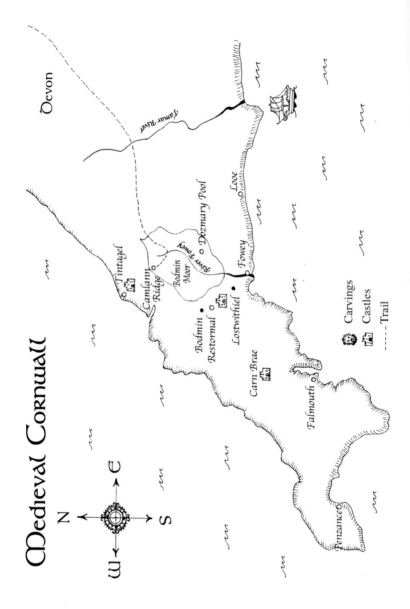

Devon

Tamar River

Tintagel

Camlann Ridge

Dozmary Pool

Bodmin Moor

River Fowey

Loe

Bodmin

Restormel

Lostwithiel

Fowey

Carn Brae

Falmouth

Penzance

N
E
S
W

Carvings
Castles
Trail

# Part One

## The Sea-Warrior

Follow the winds,
Follow the waves.
Over the sea,
To the end of our days.

Into the blue,
Where the seagulls cry.
Forward to battle,
Forward to die.

Follow the winds,
Follow the waves.
Over the sea,
To the end of our days.

# 1. The Lord of the Sea

*~ What man can master the wind and the waves? ~*

On they came, ever onward, through the sea mist that had enveloped the Cornish coast. A host of black-sailed warships; their thrusting prows smashing against the rising waves like wooden fists. Armed for battle they were, armed and ready for war!

Their prey lay before them; a ragged band of Cornish ships hastily sent out to defend the coast against this unstoppable force. At sight of the Cornish enemy, voices suddenly rang out through the black fleet and as the sailors hollered out the names of their warships in their strange tongue, the men on board The Hawk, The Falcon, The Kestrel and The Eagle prepared for battle.

Sails were tied fast, provisions were lashed down, armour was fastened, crossbows were loaded and swords were drawn. Finally, their banners were unfurled, black and silver stripes rippling in the sea-grey gloom and then, as one, they fell upon the unfortunate Cornish fleet.

The battle was swift and violent. The dark warships were far stronger than the Cornish vessels and they burst amongst them like ravaging wolves. The men on board the black fleet fought with a cold, hard strength that soon turned the encounter into a one-sided affair. And then they unleashed a new menace.

From the back of the black fleet, a huge ship suddenly pushed forward to attack. 'L' Ombre', she was called, *The Shadow*, and as soon as she had a clear view of the enemy, a violent explosion erupted from her deck and a torrent of fire was spat forth onto the Cornish fleet like a dragon's breath. 'Greek fire' the ancients named it; a lethal mixture of lime and naptha, a secret recipe of death and destruction, known only to a handful of men.

But someone on board *The Shadow* knew how to mix the deadly concoction and the mighty catapult that stood upon the deck of the ship now took command of the sea. Again and again great chunks of fire were hurled from the beast and sent crashing down upon the Cornish ships. Timbers cracked, sails burnt, oars splintered and men were sent screaming overboard as the flaming missiles showered down like meteors from hell.

One by one the Cornish warships fell. Those that had avoided the great catapult had only found themselves rammed or boarded by the other black ships. Arrows flew through the sky, swords clashed, pikes were thrust and maces whirled. The Cornishmen fought bravely to a man, but it was hopeless. Outnumbered, outshot and outmanoeuvred the end came swiftly and as

the night approached the last Cornish warship sank beneath the waves.

The man standing amidst the chaos on the prow of the flagship of the dark armada was Robert Guiscard, the Count of Brittany. 'Le Mateau', his people called him, *The Hammer*, but now the sailors and crossbowmen, the men-at-arms and the knights that stood up, bloodied and victorious, cheered a new name for their leader. In the squall of the sea, through the wind and the rain, they shouted out, "Seigneur de la mer, Seigneur de la mer" ... the Lord of the Sea.

On the shore, two survivors from the Cornish fleet dragged themselves up onto the rocks. The first man pulled himself to safety, but the second man felt his fingers slip on the seaweed. His comrade turned to him and grabbed his hand, trying desperately to pull him out from the clutches of the sea. The sailor's face bobbed under the waves and then up again. He spat out a mouthful of water and then with one last effort of life he shouted out to his companion, "Go, find a horse and ride as fast as you can to him. Tell him the Bretons are here and tell him to run. Run and hide on the moors...no-one can stop them!" With that his fingers slipped through his friend's grip like the untying of a knot and he fell back under the waves forever.

The sailor looked down into the dark blue emptiness and then he stared far out to sea. On the horizon he saw the victorious Breton fleet move ominously closer and closer to the shore, their many sails blocking out the light of the moon itself, and then he turned away from the coast and ran!

# 2. Rough Tor

*~ Those that brave the moors, are brave indeed ~*

It was late spring on the wastes of Bodmin Moor and a clear, fresh greenness filled the wide grassland. All around the bracken was unfurling, vibrant heathers danced on the moorland and golden clusters of daffodils nodded obediently in the swift morning breeze.

High up on Rough Tor, gangs of hungry seagulls fell to the earth like rain as they searched desperately for fresh food and amongst the stony outcrops, rabbits chased each other playfully as the sun arched overhead. Further down the slopes, a graceful heron swooped low and followed the course of the River Fowey southwards, through the rugged moors, and down to the Cornish coast and the open sea.

But suddenly, the calm was broken as the echoes of hooves thundered through the air. The rabbits fled back underground and the gulls scattered into the sky as a troop of horsemen crossed the horizon.

They were moving fast. Tall, black shadows against the sun. As they reached the top of the Tor, rays of golden sun fell upon them and the iron shafts of their spears shimmered like ice. They stood quite still, illuminated only for a brief moment whilst their two banners fluttered in the wind. The first one was well known; the white cross of the Duchy of Cornwall. But the other banner was more striking. Upon a green background, a beautiful golden tree bounced joyfully, as the flag rippled on the breeze. It was the banner of the valiant Sir William d'Vert, though he was better known as the Green Knight.

From out of the sunshine, another lone horseman sped across the moor. He looked ragged, exhausted and desperate and when he pulled up his horse in front of the band of warrior-knights he fell from his saddle.

A young knight jumped to the ground and helped the horseman to his feet. A salt sea air hung around the ragged man, but he raised his head long enough to utter a few sparse words to Sir William, then he fell to his knees in exhaustion.

The Green Knight immediately gazed southwards to the coast, his steel-grey eyes searching the far horizon with a look of concern. Then he turned back to his band of loyal followers and he smiled. He would make his last stand here on the moors and if he was to be defeated then at least it would be amongst noble men and stout friends!

# 3. Starlight
### ~Swift in speed is a happy steed~

"Come on Starlight," Hickory whispered in the silver-grey horse's ear as they sped across the vast open meadow. "Come on!"

About a hundred yards in front of them was a wooden pole and a cluster of red ribbons fluttered upon it like flickering flames. Hickory and the horse stared straight ahead and raced towards it, whilst behind them, a large crowd cheered and six other horses and their riders chased in hot pursuit.

But the trailing pack had no chance of catching them, for the green boy and the silver horse moved as one. Then, with a whoop of exhilaration, Hickory rounded the marker pole and entered the final stretch for home.

"Go on lad!" Nathaniel shouted excitedly from the crowd as Fern gripped his arm in anticipation. " If he can win this we're nearly there!" the old man exclaimed.

Seconds later, in a flurry of hooves, Hickory and Starlight broke through the finishing tape to a round of cheers.

It was the third race that Hickory and Starlight had won that day and the bag of coins that Nathaniel held was getting full. "Nearly enough," the old man muttered, as Hickory handed over the latest winnings.

The Horse Fair at Okehampton, on the edge of Dartmoor, had proved most successful. And Starlight, the horse stolen from the Sherrif's stables back in Nottingham the previous month, had turned out to be a splendid racehorse.

"One more race should do it," Nathaniel stated, carefully putting the coins back in the bag. For even though they were barely twelve miles from the River Tamar and the border with Cornwall, they did not yet have all the toll money they needed. But Fern and Hickory were not listening to the old man, they were too busy staring at the mob of burly locals who were marching toward them. Realising the danger, Hickory put his fingers to his mouth and whistled and from the patch of tall grass where they were grazing, Starlight and two other horses trotted quickly over.

As Hickory leapt upon Starlight's back, Fern alerted Nathaniel to the impending trouble and they grabbed their knapsacks and cloaks from under a willow tree and hurriedly mounted their own steeds.

The gang of locals saw that the three

strange outsiders were making their escape, and began to run toward them, pulling cudgels and knives from their belts. But as they closed upon the riders, Starlight stood up upon its hind legs and thundered its hooves down upon the ground. The men drew back and with another whistle Hickory drew up the reins and Starlight leapt clean over the bramble hedge that blocked their path to freedom.

Fern and Nathaniel held on tight as their mounts did the same. As the villagers cursed and swore, the three riders sped away across the open fields of south Devon.

"That was close!" Nathaniel gasped, as the horses pulled up in the lower reaches of the Tamar Valley.

"Bad losers!" replied Hickory. "They shouldn't let us take part, if they won't let us keep our winnings!"

"Agreed, lad. You won fair and square. And yet we don't have enough money for the toll. I can't see how we can get any more before the border. We may have twenty silver pennies, but we need at least thirty!"

"Perhaps the toll-keeper will let us off," Fern

suggested hopefully.

"Perhaps pigs will fly!" huffed Nathaniel.

"Well statues can!" grinned Hickory, reminding Nathaniel of his friend, the Lincoln Imp. "So, who knows?"

The old man smiled at the memory and at the ever-hopeful nature of his two young companions.

So with more faith in their hearts than cash in their pockets, they rode on down to the river, and on to Cornwall.

# 4. The Toll-keeper

*~The River of life begins with a gurgle~*

"Well, there it is." Nathaniel pointed across the swelling Tamar River to the tree-lined bank on the far side. "Cornwall, the far tip of England. A land gripped by the sea, a land of tin and smugglers, a land of dark moors and windswept bays."

"So why does your King Henry not rule there?" Fern asked, as she followed Nathaniel and Hickory down the track to the riverside.

"Cornwall is the last realm of the Celts; a proud and independent people, with their own language, customs and of course their own ruler. And though the ruler of Cornwall pays homage to the King of England, in Cornwall he is Lord and Master!"

"So the Green Knight is like the King of Cornwall?" Hickory's voice rose with excitement.

"I suppose so," Nathaniel answered. "Though it's a little more complicated than that."

For the next few hours they followed the curves and bends of the river, as its trail led them along the valley floor. It was boggy, and the hooves of their ponies splashed loudly where the banks of the Tamar had flooded with the spring thaw.

There were no willow trees to swing over on here and the river was far too deep and too fast to swim across. Besides, they would need their horses in Cornwall. So for the next hour, as the sun began to fall, they searched for the toll-keeper's moorings.

It was almost dusk by the time they spotted the wooden raft that was tied up by the small jetty. The vessel lay empty and for a moment they thought about taking it and crossing the border without having to pay at all. But they knew that would mean leaving the boat on the far shore, and as the toll-keeper would not be able to get it back again, they dismissed the notion.

And then, the horses reared up in surprise. From the toll-keeper's cottage that sat nestled by the riverside, cries of pain suddenly rang out!

Tying their horses by the moorings, the three travellers crossed to the tiny dwelling, and tentatively, Nathaniel knocked on the cottage door. After a long delay, an ashen-faced man opened it.

"We heard the crying," Nathaniel stated. "Is there anything we can do to help?"

"It's my wife," the man replied anxiously,

"she is giving birth."

"I see," said Nathaniel.

"But there is something wrong!" the man continued.

"What is it?" Fern stepped forward.

The toll-keeper was in such a state, he didn't even notice the colour of her skin. "I…I don't know for sure," he stuttered, "but I think the baby is the wrong way around."

"A breach birth," Nathaniel stated, "only ever seen one before!"

"Then you know what to do?" The toll-keeper's voice was desperate.

"Hardly. It was a horse and her foal!"

"But the principle is the same, Nathaniel." Fern added. Then she took control of the situation swiftly. She entered the cottage, spotted the woman in the far corner of the room, and strode over to the bed with purpose.

As the others entered behind her, Fern knelt by the toll-keeper's wife and lay her hand upon the woman's brow. "What is your name?" she asked, gently.

"Sarah," the toll-keeper's wife gasped.

"Well Sarah, everything is going to be fine."

Fern looked to her brother and waved him over to her side. "Hickory, go outside and find me some *Olurus*."

The toll-keeper looked bewildered. "What

can I do to help?" His eyes pleaded with Fern.

"Go with my brother and find some plants for me," she replied.

"What is it you need?" the toll-keeper's face beamed, glad at last he could do something practical to help his wife.

"'Feverfew' you call it. Also, as we tied the horses I noticed a small tree with white flowers."

"It was a guelder rose," said Nathaniel, "though some people call it swamp elder, because it likes the wet conditions, such as the riverside. In autumn, it has little red berries."

"Well the bark is very useful. It will help ease the pain in Sarah's stomach muscles."

"I always wondered why it was nick-named crampbark," Nathaniel smiled.

"Well, now you know!" Fern answered him and then turned back to the toll-keeper. "When you have found the bark, stoke up that fire," Fern pointed to the pathetic cluster of damp logs that was sizzling in the hearth, "and boil up some water. Plenty of it." She finished giving orders and returned her attention to Sarah, whose breathing was now coming in loud, sharp breaths.

Nathaniel ushered the toll-keeper toward the doorway and out of harm's way.

"She will look after her won't she?" the man's worried face looked back to his wife who gave out another cry of pain.

"If she can't help her, no-one can!"
Nathaniel answered and then he closed the door.

⚜⚜⚜

Outside the cottage, Hickory and the toll-keeper
sat in silence, staring idly at the meandering river.
Every now and then cries would tear the
quietness apart and the toll-keeper would stare
back at the door and tighten his knuckles. But he
knew that inside the old man and the strange girl
were doing all they could.

It had been two hours since they had boiled
up the crampbark and made a feverfew tea and it
had been another hour since the old man had
closed the cottage door and told them to wait.
The evening drew close now. The wind dropped
and the birds' chatter died down. On the
riverbank a heron poked about in the flooded
shallows, hunting for stranded fish. Further
downstream, Hickory spotted two otters playing
in the mud. The noise alerted the toll-keeper, but
in the half-light he could not see as well as
Hickory.

"Hope it's not a Bucca Boo!" he murmured
as he watched the riverside carefully.

"A what?" asked Hickory.

"A Bucca Boo. It's a Cornish goblin.
Sometimes they cross the river and steal sheep."

"Well, it's not!" Hickory smiled. "It's just a couple of playful otters."

"You have good eyes," the toll-keeper stared at Hickory as if he had just noticed him for the first time. "Strange looking aren't you?"

"So they say!" Hickory smiled back.

"Tell me," the toll-keeper whispered, "why do you want to go to Cornwall?"

"We are looking for the Green Knight," Hickory replied, "we think he may be our father."

"I see," the toll-keeper pondered the boy's reply.

"Is he actually green?" Hickory's voice grew anxious.

"I've never seen him, I'm afraid," the toll-keeper answered. "He spends most of his time up in his high tower at Tintagel. Besides, I only visit Cornwall for a few brief minutes to drop my passengers off."

"Well, our hope is that he is green like us. You see we have been looking for our father for a long time."

"Then perhaps he is. You and your sister both have a lordly feel about you," the toll-keeper patted Hickory's shoulder.

Hickory looked back down the river, toward the playing otters and he smiled a hopeful smile.

Suddenly, from inside the cottage, the cries of pain, which had peppered their conversation, abruptly stopped. The toll-keeper stood up from the riverbank and his eyes stared toward the door of the tiny dwelling. He did not know what to do! Had something dreadful happened inside? Why had his wife stopped crying?

And then he laughed as he heard the sound he had been waiting for. The sound he had been praying for. The sound of a new-born baby testing its lungs.

"She's found her voice, then," Nathaniel stated as he watched Fern wrap the baby in a woollen blanket.

"It would seem so," Fern replied with a grin.

"Is there no end to your skills?" The old man smiled at his young friend, whilst she held the new-born baby aloft.

"Patience and nature do most of the work, Nathaniel. Although, I seem to know a lot more about the uses of plants and herbs than your people."

"You certainly do!" the old man replied. "I shall never look at swamp elder in the same way again!"

Fern had just taken the baby and nestled her on the bed next to her mother, when the toll-keeper burst excitedly through the door. He stood there for a moment and took in the scene before him, checking that everyone was okay. Then he sprinted across the floor of the cottage and knelt down by the bedside.

"Oh Sarah," he gasped and he kissed his wife gently on the forehead. "She's perfect!" he whispered, as he stroked the baby's dark curls.

"She looks like you, Samuel," Sarah gazed up at her husband.

"Poor child!" laughed the toll-keeper.

At the other end of the room, Fern washed out the bedclothes and cleared away her herbal potions. She sang whilst she worked and her voice filled the tiny cottage, and brought laughter to them all.

"I would like to name her after you," Sarah smiled, looking over at the green girl. "What is your name?"

Fern stopped what she was doing and joined them by the bedside. She stared at the tiny bundle before them. "My name is Fern," she replied, without thinking.

But as she returned back to her cleaning and her singing, she suddenly halted in mid-tune.

"What's wrong?" asked Sarah.

"Oh nothing," Fern replied, "try to get some sleep."

Sarah smiled at her husband, closed her eyes

and rolled over, so she did not see the anguish that fell upon Fern's face.

But my real name is *Clyssa*, Fern thought sadly.

# 5. Cornwall

*~ A land of tors, cliffs and mists, a land where magic still exists~*

The raft trip across the Tamar to Cornwall took barely a quarter of an hour, but the weary travellers sat aboard the vessel in quiet reflection.

Nathaniel, sitting at the front of the raft, thought back to the long ride down from the great Forest of Sherwood. He closed his eyes for a brief moment and remembered fondly the pastries he had eaten in Derbyshire and the cider he had drunk in Somerset.

Fern, holding the reins of the three horses at the back of the raft, stood, lost in a daydream. How long since we had left Suffolk, she thought to herself? How long had we been stuck in Lincoln? When did we leave Robin Hood behind? Time was slipping through her fingers, time away from her homeland, time away from her trees, and time away from her father.

But, unlike his sister and the old man, Hickory did not look backward. He stood next to the toll-keeper, watching him push his pole into the river and punt them slowly across. Too slowly, thought Hickory. He was so keen to touch Cornish ground and find the Green Knight, that all other feelings deserted him. All his thoughts were bent toward finding the warrior, who he hoped was his father.

"This is the furthest west I have ever been," Nathaniel thought aloud, as he stepped off the raft. "I have travelled as far east as Jerusalem, nearly two thousand miles, but I have never been as far west, as I am now."

"And further west you must go too!" the toll-keeper stated cheerfully, "if you want to find your Green Knight, that is."

"True," replied Nathaniel, reaching for his bag of coins.

"Now, how much do we owe you? We have only twenty silver pennies, I'm afraid."

The toll-keeper laughed. "You don't owe me a single penny. It is I who's indebted to you."

"That is very kind," Fern replied.

"Now take this here, before I forget it," the toll-keeper said, handing over a wicker basket.

"Sarah has put inside a loaf of bread and a Devon Oke. It's a cheese made from Devonshire milk, the best there is!"

"Thank you," said Fern.

"Thank *you*," replied the toll-keeper earnestly. "And remember there is always a safe haven for you here if you need it. Now, I must get back to my girls."

Pushing the raft off, and jumping aboard, he gave a wave of his hand and within a few minutes he was on his way back to Devon.

"Come on then!" cried Hickory as he mounted Starlight. "Let's get a move on!"

They rode quickly, across great swathes of open farmland, passing by the tiny villages of Yeolmbridge, Tregeare, and St Clether. Then, as the rich farmland ran out, they found themselves upon a wide, open heathland.

Suddenly, below the hooves of their horses, were ridges of granite, and in places the earth grew wet and boggy. The horses were forced to slow down now, and pick their way carefully through the rock and the mires. It was bleak and barren here, and it seemed to Hickory as if they had just set foot upon the moon itself. But if they had studied the maps of Cornwall, they would have seen that they were on the northern edge of Bodmin Moor. A wild and rugged land, steeped in myths and legends.

They halted briefly on an outcrop of stone, and watched a Meadow Brown butterfly dance around a patch of purple heather. Then, Hickory

spotted a line of figures on the far horizon, so they dismounted from their horses and crept to the edge of the rocks to spy upon them.

They watched closely and soon saw that the figures were all carrying great longbows. They moved fast, constantly looking behind them, as if they were worried about being followed.

Then there was a loud thunder of hooves at the back of the line of bowmen, and a pack of horsemen appeared upon the moor. They spotted the archers, and as one, the pack of mounted knights drew their blades and fell upon them.

In a swirl of swords, the knights cut the bowmen to the ground. Then, one of them dropped down to the floor and searched through the clothing of the dying men.

After a few moments, the knight pulled out a piece of green cloth and laughed as he saw the device upon it. He took the cloth and cleaned the blood off his blade and then he threw it on the floor. Barking out orders, in a strange tongue, he jumped back on his mount, and within minutes he led the pack of horsemen away, west.

From their hiding place behind the crags, Fern, Hickory and Nathaniel watched in terror as the pained cries of the bowmen slowly faded away.

"What was that about?" Fern turned to Nathaniel.

"I have no idea," he replied thoughtfully.

"Come on," Hickory called as he jumped onto Starlight's back. "Let's see if any of them are still alive!"

But none of them were. The horsemen had been brutally efficient in their attack; the archers lay in a bloodied heap upon the tor.

Fern quickly turned her eyes away from the awful scene. She knew it was too late to save any of the men that lay dead on the ground, so she stayed sat upon her horse, Moon-shadow. But Hickory dismounted from Starlight and bent down to search the bodies.

It was not long before he found what he wanted. Gently moving the hand of a dead archer, he picked up the green cloth that he had seen the horseman wipe his blade with. Turning it over in his hand he saw what the horseman had seen.

"What have you got there, lad?" Nathaniel asked, dismounting from his own horse, Wind-walker.

"I'm not sure," Hickory replied, "but look at this!"

Underneath the blood-stains, Hickory pointed to the symbol of a golden tree. "Seems like it's a flag or something."

Nathaniel stared at the material, deep in thought. "It is, indeed," he stated after a long pause, "it's a standard and on it seems to be the symbol of some great Lord."

"Do you think it could be . . . ?"

"I don't know, lad," Nathaniel interrupted Hickory, before he could finish his words. "But whatever it is, that cavalry captain was no friend of its owner!"

Fern suddenly pointed across the grassland, "Quick, look over there." From the height of her saddle she had spotted more figures, moving across the moors.

Hurriedly, Nathaniel and Hickory mounted their horses once again, and following Fern, they rode across the open heathland. From nowhere, they were swiftly surrounded by long lines of people moving along, as if on a pilgrimage to the shrine of some great saint.

"Where are you all going?" Nathaniel called to them.

"We are going to the Green Knight's encampment!" an old man shouted back.

The children's faces beamed, even Nathaniel smiled.

"All we need to do is just follow them," Hickory grinned.

What they didn't ask was why so many people were hurrying to the court of the Green

Knight. For if they had done, they would have found out what it was that drove them from their homes and on to the moors. It was fear! Fear of the approaching war, fear of the Breton hordes that had swept up through Cornwall. Fear that no one could protect them from the ensuing disaster.

Fern, Hickory and Nathaniel, following them blindly toward the Green Knight, knew nothing of the turmoil that was engulfing the land all around them.

"Look!" cried Hickory.

Before them, on the brow of the moor, was a huge encampment. Emerald green banners fluttered on the breeze, hundreds of green tents stood silhouetted against the sky, horsemen dressed in green surcoats, rode this way and that. And as Fern, Hickory and Nathaniel rode toward them, their hearts rose with hope.

# 6. The Green Knight
## ~ Many have died because of their pride~

**O**nce inside the gates of the encampment, Fern, Hickory and Nathaniel dismounted from their horses and led them by the reins. They were amazed at how many people were crammed into the camp. There were women chatting, babies crying, children playing and old men grumbling, but they all stopped and stared in wonder when the children passed by the ragged lines of tents.

As they walked further into the heart of the camp, they saw that most of the people here were men; men that were preparing for battle. They passed by blacksmiths mending shields, fletchers making arrows and squires cleaning armour and then there were the soldiers themselves. There were archers firing at targets, there were men-at-arms swinging swords, there were pikemen stabbing at bales of straw and there were knights jousting.

Hickory didn't know where to look first, but one thing he did stare at were all the banners that rippled from the tops of the tents. "They're the same as the one that we found on the dead archer," he whispered to Nathaniel. "The golden tree on the green background."

"I know," the old man replied, "which means that the Green Knight has enemies!"

"What have we here?" A voice interrupted their whisperings and from across the far side of the camp, a brightly dressed figure bounded over to the three of them.

"Well, bless my soul," he grinned, "this is most strange!"

"What is?" Fern asked indignantly.

"Little green people, of course!" he answered.

"But we are in the camp of the Green Knight, are we not?" Fern answered him sharply.

"We are indeed, my lady," the little fellow replied, "and I do apologise for my cheek. It's my job you see. Let me introduce myself. My name is Penfric and I am Court Jester to the Green Knight." The old fool bowed before them.

"Well, Penfric," Nathaniel snapped, "we would like an audience with your master."

"Would you now! Then follow me and I'll take you to him."

"Is he really green too?" Hickory's question burst out excitedly, as they got in step behind the little man.

"He must be!" The old jester giggled in reply. "He's called the Green Knight, isn't he?"

And though the children smiled at this, the tone of his voice made Nathaniel doubtful.

They crossed to the centre of the encampment and found themselves in front of an enormous emerald pavilion. On the sides were woven the emblem of the golden tree and two mail-shirted knights with gleaming swords barred their entry.

The old jester turned to Nathaniel and the children and grinned. "I will check if his Lordship will see you now," he said. "Wait here!"

Nathaniel and the children stood silently, deep in thought, whilst the little jester disappeared through the entrance of the Green Knight's great tent.

"My Lord, you have visitors," Penfric addressed William d'Vert, who was stood by a trestle table, studying scrolls by the light of a tall candle.

"Can they fight?" the Green Knight's mind was set upon only one course, like a ship sailing into harbour.

"I doubt it, my Lord," replied Penfric with a wry smile. "It's an old man and two children."

"No use to me then!" d'Vert mumbled gruffly and returned to studying his map.

"Yet they may be of interest, my Lord."

"Why?" the Green Knight's eyes flickered with curiosity.

"You need to see them, Sire," the jester replied.

"Don't play games with me, Penfric. I am in no mood for it!" d'Vert drew his gaze away from the table and stared at the old jester.

"Trust me, my Lord," grinned Penfric, "just

trust me."

"Very well, show them in then," d'Vert replied with a scowl.

⚜ ⚜ ⚜

"His Lordship will see you now," Penfric stated, as he held open the flap of the Green Knight's pavilion.

Hickory and Fern's anticipation grew, and although they had been twice disappointed before, it was hard to control the excitement they felt. Hickory in particular was keen to see if his father was really a Green Knight - how marvellous that would be!

They stepped inside the tent to find a crowd of knights and nobles in front of them and for a brief moment felt overwhelmed. But Nathaniel took them by the hand and led them forward and as they moved, the men parted, as if at some secret command. Then, at the end of the pavilion they saw a figure bent over a table, and as they were ushered toward him, the Green Knight looked up.

All eyes fell upon him. In the candlelight his face was as proud and as noble as an ancient king. His eyes were stern, his beard was flecked with grey and when he gazed over toward them, Hickory thought he looked as if he was carved from stone. The images of Nathaniel's green men carvings flashed through the boy's mind, but as he stared at the noble face before him, he realised that the Green Knight was not actually green! They had been disappointed once again!

"Oh no!" Fern cried, burying her face in Nathaniel's shoulder.

"Good heavens!" William d'Vert said in surprise. "I don't usually have this effect on people."

"We were hoping that you would be green," Hickory stared up at d'Vert through watery eyes.

"Green?" d'Vert laughed. But then he saw the colour of the children's skin and suddenly looked shocked himself. "Oh my God!" he declared loudly. "What are you?"

"They are children, my Lord," Nathaniel addressed William d'Vert calmly. "They are lost children and they . . ." the old man paused, "we... had hoped that you might have been their father."

"I see," d'Vert, replied. "Then, I am sorry that your journey has come to nothing. You see I am only known as the Green Knight because of my name - Vert is the French word for green, you see. My ancestors decided that our coat-of-arms should match our name and thus we wear green livery."

"I understand," Fern replied sadly.

"It's a disappointment, all the same,"

Nathaniel spoke in a tired voice, as the children slumped against him with exhaustion.

"You look done in," d'Vert stated. "Come, sit down and tell me your tale." He drew them toward the fire that blazed in the centre of the tent. "Though it must be quick," he continued, "we have plans to make and defences to shape. If you hadn't already noticed, war has come to Cornwall."

It was Nathaniel who told the Green Knight and his court of their quest. Fern and Hickory sat in silence on the floor at the old man's feet. They stared gloomily at the flickering flames, lost in their sorrow, lost in their thoughts and lost in their hearts.

"Come, don't be so sad," d'Vert knelt down by the children and spoke gently to them. "I realise you are disappointed, but you have arrived here for a reason. I am sure of that."

"What do you mean?" Hickory suddenly snapped out from his daydream and stared at d'Vert.

"Well, green children appearing at the Green Knight's court on the eve of battle. Surely that is a sign of some sort. An omen!"

Some of the knights around d'Vert nodded their agreement, though others looked more sceptical. How could these two odd children help them defeat the entire Breton army?

"After all," d'Vert continued, "we are in Arthur's land, here. A land of magic and mystery! A land where anything can happen!"

"Who's Arthur?" Hickory asked him, though it was Nathaniel who answered him.

*"Go seek the King in Avalon or down the cliffs of Wales."*

"He does that," said Hickory, looking toward Nathaniel, "bits of old poems and ancient songs. I don't think he can remember the whole thing though - too old I suppose!"

The old man chuckled, but then d'Vert finished the lines for him, *"Through Cornwall and through Brittany, his legend still prevails."*

"Not you too!" cried Hickory.

D'Vert laughed, "It is an old ballad about King Arthur."

"So, who was he?" Hickory asked again.

"Arthur was the King of the Britons, who defended the land from evil. He led his band of brave knights on many dangerous quests; they were known as the Knights of the Round Table. Helped by his wife, Queen Guinevere, and his friend the wizard, Merlin, Arthur's virtuous Kingdom reigned for a brief time," Nathaniel stated.

"It is said that his court of Camelot was here in Cornwall," d'Vert continued, "and not far from here he fought his last battle against his mortal enemy Mordred."

"Was he killed in the battle?" Hickory asked.

"So the legend has it, though some say Arthur will return one day, to save Britain again."

"When he lay dying," Penfric added, "he asked one of his knights to throw his sword 'Excalibur' into Dozmary pool, to the south of here. It was said that the lady of the lake reached up her hand and took the magic sword back into the waters, where it still lies, awaiting his return."

Hickory's eyes widened in wonder at the legend of the mythical King.

"Now, enough of ancient heroes," D'Vert's eyes rested back on his jester. "Penfric here, will take you to the cooks for something to eat and then he will find you a tent. You all look as if you need a good night's rest. We will talk again in the morning."

D'Vert turned back to his nobles and his maps and the business of war and the aged jester showed them out of the great pavilion.

After a warm supper, they retired to their tent and made themselves comfortable amongst the blankets that they had found upon the floor. It was not long before Nathaniel had started snoring peacefully and Fern had put aside her disappointment and slipped into her dreams. But

Hickory lay wide awake. He kept thinking of the noble knights that were standing so tall in the Green Knight's tent. Their shining armour, their sharp swords, their warlike bearing, their battered shields...

# 7. The Company of Excalibur

*~ Warriors bound by trust, lie together in the dust~*

At daybreak, after a breakfast of tasteless oat porridge, Penfric showed the newcomers around the Green Knight's encampment. Whilst they wandered through the ragged army's settlement, the first thing they noticed was the hastily dug ditch which surrounded the site to deter attack. At the top of the ditch was a ring of sharpened wooden stakes that stuck out like a line of enormous hedgehogs.

"The Ancient Romans did this each night they camped in enemy territory," Penfric claimed.

"Each soldier carried a spade and a wooden stake along with his weapons and armour," Nathaniel replied knowledgeably. "The Romans ruled the greatest empire the west had ever seen and it was the army that carved it out for them."

But as Nathaniel surveyed the rest of the Cornish army encampment, he could see no other comparison with the might and organisation of the Romans. Here stood a desperate band of warriors on a last stand. It was only the will of the Green Knight that kept them together. A powerful man, Nathaniel thought, as he watched d'Vert step from his tent and bark orders at the men around him. Just how far would he go to keep his land?

They carried on walking until the old jester stopped in front of a small tent on the northern side of the encampment and turned to the three of them. "Well, this is where I will leave you. His Lordship asked me to deliver you into the hands of someone nearer your own age," and with that he smiled, winked and returned to d'Vert's side.

Nathaniel and the children stood, watching the tent before them, and then a young man of about fifteen years of age appeared. He had not seen them standing there, so he carried on with his tasks. He sat down on the far side of the tent and drew his sword, took a cloth from the ground and oiled and polished the blade. He stroked the weapon carefully as if he was caressing a pet and then he stood up again.

The three of them stared on in silence as the lad, silhouetted against the dawn sky, proceeded to thrust and parry in battle with an invisible enemy. Then, after a few minutes of this shadow fighting, the young warrior spied them and halted his swordplay.

"Good morning!" Nathaniel smiled at the lad.

"Good morning to you!" the young man replied. "So it's true then?" he continued.

"What is?" asked Hickory.

"That green children have appeared to help us defeat the Bretons and save the Green Knight!"

"I don't know about that!" Fern replied crossly.

"It is just what the men have been saying! I meant no offence." The young man put down his sword and crossed over to them.

"I'm sorry," Fern smiled at the young warrior. "It's just that we have journeyed far only to be frustrated once again."

"I understand," the lad replied, "Penfric told me that you hoped d'Vert was your father."

"Yes, it would have been wonderful to have been the son of such a knight as him," said Hickory.

"Would it?" the lad asked thoughtfully.

"Of course!" Hickory retorted.

"He is your father isn't he?" Fern was staring carefully at the young man.

"Yes," he answered, "he is. Let me introduce myself. I am Ethan d'Vert, the son of the Green Knight and heir to the Duchy of Cornwall. At least what's left of it! Which appears to be just this stretch of miserable moorland!"

Hickory looked stunned and Nathaniel stared at the boy with fresh wonder.

"How did you guess he was my father?" Ethan turned to meet Fern's gaze.

"You have the same eyes,"she replied, "sea-blue and full of pride."

"My father is a proud man, you are right. Too proud perhaps!" Ethan replied solemnly.

"Tell me, young man," Nathaniel sat down next to Ethan d'Vert's tent, "how did this war begin?"

"That is a long story," the lad answered, thoughtfully.

"So start at the beginning," Nathaniel smiled.

"Well, Robert Guiscard, the Count of Brittany, and now it would seem most of Cornwall, is my father's half-brother."

The children sat down next to Nathaniel and all three of them listened intently to the tale.

"My grandmother was first married to my grand-father Thomas d'Vert and that was when my father was born. But when Thomas died, my grandmother married Roger Guiscard of Brittany and a year later she gave birth to Robert."

"I see," mumbled Nathaniel.

"At first there were no problems," Ethan d'Vert continued. "Cornwall and Brittany have always been linked by common bonds such as the sea and the language, and now it was linked by blood. My father and Robert even used to play together as boys! "

"So what happened?" asked Fern.

"A woman happened!" Ethan answered. "My father fell in love."

"Ah," murmured Nathaniel, guessing the ending to the tale.

"You see, the trouble was, the lady in question was already betrothed to Robert. So she and my father ran away together and were married. My father and Robert have feuded ever since."

"How long has this been going on?" Nathaniel asked.

"Seventeen long and bitter years," Ethan answered.

"But the war has only just begun!" Fern stated.

"Yes, it escalated from a fishing dispute and because neither my father or Guiscard would back down, it has come to this."

"So, men die, villages are burnt and children are left homeless, all because of a few shoals of fish?" Fern looked angry.

"I am afraid so," Ethan's eyes looked to the floor.

"They die because of your father's pride!" Fern replied.

"I know," Ethan remained downcast, "but my father will not take advice from me. Or anyone else for that matter. And if he cannot be dissuaded from war then it is my duty to follow him."

"So who was this woman that set them at each other's throats?" Nathaniel asked.

"Her name is Lady Eliza and at present she is safe in Tintagel castle, high up on the rocks. Oh!" he paused for a moment, "and she is also my mother!"

"Once you join, only death can release you!"

Hickory's face was serious, as William d'Vert addressed the assembled group of knights around him. "Tonight, I ask you to pledge a solemn oath that you will follow me into battle and stand fast against our enemy." The grim-faced men nodded their agreement and knelt down before the Green Knight, and a death-like silence filled the great tent.

It was midnight, and Hickory had been roused from his sleep and brought to this secret ceremony whilst the rest of the camp slept. As the candles flickered in the half-light of the tent, Hickory had watched, as one by one the Green Knight's most trusted noblemen were brought before him.

Once they were all there, d'Vert had begun to address them. "Our brave band of brothers will be called the Company of Excalibur," he continued, "in honour of King Arthur's magical sword that served him so ably."

The noblemen cheered. "And so it will be you as members of the Company, that will lead the men of Cornwall against the Bretons. It will be you that must hold firm when lesser men waver. It will be you that will charge upon the enemy, though you be outnumbered and all hope is lost!"

The Green Knight stopped speaking and looked each man in the eye, searching for signs of weakness and when he found none, he gripped each man's hand in turn and their defiant pact was made.

All the while the ceremony continued, Hickory held the Green Knight's standard, and he smiled with pride as the Company was formed. For was he not one of them? Was he not ready to give his life for his Lord?

Then, as silently as they had come, each knight rose from their knees and returned to their slumber. "He'll kill us all!" one of the knights mumbled as he left the tent. But Hickory ignored him, for his heart burst with pride and his mind rippled with the glory of war!

And with those thoughts running through his head he slipped back into his own tent, past his sleeping sister and his snoring old friend, and climbed back into his bed. And the ceremony of the Company of Excalibur drifted away like a dream!

# 8. A Call to Arms
## ~ Take sword and shield, quiver and bow
## It's off to battle, we must go~

**B**y the following morning, the mood across the camp was expectant and as d'Vert awaited news of the Breton advance, it seemed as if all minds were drawn to that singular purpose.

At midday, Penfric sought to ease the tension and raise the spirits of the army. So whilst the knights and squires, the foot soldiers and the archers, the camp followers and Nathaniel and the children sat to eat, the old jester began to entertain them.

He stood up on one of the trestle tables that stood by the camp kitchen and as the rows of soldiers and their camp followers turned to face him, he began to tell some well-known Cornish tales.

The first yarn he told was of a farmer's son called Jack, who lived near Land's End in the days of King Arthur. Nearby, lived a giant called Cormoran, who terrorised the land by eating cattle and sheep and sometimes even people! At this the children around Penfric's feet gasped! A reward was offered for anyone who could slay this fearsome giant and Jack duly took up the challenge. He went out one day and dug a huge pit and then covered it with sticks and straw. Then, he lured the giant to him by blowing his hunting horn.

The noise incensed Cormoran and he ran toward Jack, only to fall down into the great pit. Quickly, Jack took out his pick-axe, and killed the giant. The children below Penfric suddenly cheered and the soldiers laughed.

Then, Penfric continued, Jack covered the pit with earth and went to claim his reward – a beautiful gold sword. So, Jack became a hero and the land was saved from the wicked giant but, Penfric's voice softened to a whisper, it is said that if you pass by the pit, you can sometimes hear a moaning noise, reverberating up from the earth!

The crowd around the old jester applauded and then he told more tales of the fairy folk that inhabit Cornwall. The mischievous piskies, the devilish spriggans and the mine-dwelling knockers.

The crowd knew these stories, but it was good to hear them again for they were Cornish tales and it reminded them that this was their land. When the old jester had finished, a tall knight rose from the tables and in a deep, hearty voice he sang the old Song of the West. As he began, others soon joined in and by the end of the song all the crowd were on their feet.

## The Song of the West

*We cast our nets,*
*and fish our seas.*
*Our sails catch,*
*the morning breeze.*

*This western land is our home,*
*Cornishmen don't need to roam.*

*We mine for tin,*
*And dig down deep.*
*We climb the cliffs,*
*that are so steep.*

*This western land is our home,*
*Cornishmen don't need to roam.*

*We walk the moors,*
*and farm the land.*
*West of the Tamar,*
*is where we stand.*

*This western land is our home,*
*Cornishmen don't need to roam.*

As the singing ended, a horseman appeared outside the encampment. High up on the brow of the moor, he swung his horse toward the tented city and galloped down to it.

The guards at the entrance signalled to him as he passed by them and then the messenger rode swiftly through the gates and across the camp to halt in front of d'Vert's great pavilion. Penfric ran inside to find the Green Knight and within minutes he appeared at the tent's doorway.

"Tintagel is safe my Lord," the messenger called out to d'Vert, whilst he dismounted.

"Thank heavens for that," d'Vert exclaimed. "Eliza is safe," he repeated to himself. "Do you hear that Ethan? Your mother is safe!" he smiled over to his son.

"But that is the only good news, Sire," the messenger continued. "The Breton army has crossed the River Fowey."

"Oh no!" exclaimed one of d'Vert's knights, as everyone listened to the messenger's bad tidings.

"What news of the towns and castles?" shouted another warrior.

The rider looked downcast. "Lostwithiel has fallen and Carn Brea too," he said glumly.

The crowd sighed; Carn Brea and Lostwithiel had been strong fortresses.

"And what of Restormel?" the Green Knight barked.

The messenger could not bear to look the Green Knight in the face. "Ranulf de Roche has lost Restormel Castle, my Lord."

"Damn!" d'Vert roared.

"Everywhere they go, they burn and pillage!

All of Cornwall is in flames, Lord," the messenger's face looked tired . . . beaten.

William d'Vert looked to the heavens above.

"So it has come to this," he lamented, "I have become a fugitive in my own land, with these Breton dogs snapping at my heels!"

"What will you do father?" Ethan asked.

The Green Knight paused in thought for a moment. "We will meet at the Whispering Knights," he replied, "call all men of Cornwall to arms," and he stormed back into his tent.

"What are the Whispering Knights?" asked Fern.

"They are nine great standing stones," it was Penfric that answered her, "it's said that they were once knights plotting to help Mordred defeat King Arthur. The wizard, Merlin, turned them all to stone. It has long been a meeting place for the Dukes of Cornwall. A rallying place to gather men to fight."

"But why can't your father ask for peace?" Fern turned to face Ethan d'Vert with a scowl upon her face. "Surely a treaty could still be forged with these Bretons?"

"My father is too proud to back down," Ethan replied.

"Even if it means the loss of many lives?" she answered crossly.

"I fear so. He believes he is right, so he will

not yield. Not till he drives the Bretons back to the sea," Ethan paused for a moment, "or until he dies fighting!"

"So we are going to war!" Hickory's excitement was all too obvious.

"No!" said Fern. "I want nothing to do with it!"

"We should be moving on," Nathaniel agreed. "We still have your father to find. You have not forgotten that, have you Hickory?"

"No, but I am a brother in the Company of Excalibur now, honour-bound to his Lordship. I cannot leave him when he needs me."

"What?" Nathaniel looked furious.

"I joined last night. It was a secret ceremony," Hickory answered with pride.

"What use are you to him?" Fern asked her brother with growing frustration.

"I am his lucky charm. He cannot lose a battle with me holding his standard."

"Don't be so stupid, Hickory! He is not your father, he has no hold upon you. We must leave!"

"I fear the only safe place to be now, is with the Green Knight's army anyway, Fern," Ethan d'Vert interrupted. "The Bretons are rampaging all over Cornwall. There is no escape from this moor at present. Guiscard has sealed the county and is closing in upon us. It may be that you will have to fight your way out with the rest of us."

He looked at her and then bowed his head. "I am afraid, we are all trapped!"

# 9. The Whispering Knights
## ~ In ancient stones, legends roam ~

It was not far to the appointed meeting place for the Green Knight's army to march to. But even so, with the movement of such a mass of people and equipment, it was well past noon by the time they approached the Whispering Knights.

There was not a sound upon the moors. Not a single bird was singing. No rabbits played, no butterflies danced and no deer skipped past. And Fern noticed this more keenly than anyone else. It disturbed her. She knew that some fear, some foreboding lay upon the creatures, and perhaps even the very land around them. Something dreadful was going to happen, something that she had no power to stop, and it frightened her.

She turned to Nathaniel who was riding alongside her at the rear of the snaking army. His presence comforted her, as always. But when she looked for Hickory, she was dismayed to see him riding at the head of the soldiers and chatting merrily with Penfric, the knights and William d'Vert.

Up at the front, now dressed in the livery of the Green Knight, Hickory was the first to spot the ancient ring of standing stones. "Look Sire," he stated, and he quickly pointed them out to his new master. William d'Vert smiled as he recognised the tall, dark, distant shapes.

The knights at the front suddenly cheered as they all caught sight of the stone circle, high on the western edge of Bodmin moor. Then, as one, with the permission of d'Vert, the Company of Excalibur, galloped up to the meeting place. Hickory, eager to be involved, gave chase with Starlight and before long he had caught up with the leading pack of knights. From behind, William d'Vert laughed, as the green boy now passed the pack and led the way up to the stones.

"A good omen, indeed!" he shouted to Penfric and the little jester, bobbing along on his old pony, grinned in reply.

By the time the rest of the army had caught up with Hickory, he'd had time to give the Whispering Knights a closer inspection. Undoubtedly from a distance, standing tall and proud, the stones really had looked like the Whispering Knights, from which they received their name. But up close, the stones stood quiet and lifeless.

"You can't bring these to life, then?" Nathaniel laughed as he climbed down from

Wind-walker and reminded Hickory of his friend the Lincoln Imp.

"No," Hickory replied with a smile, "I don't think there was ever any life in these stones. Besides, if they were knights of Mordred and therefore the enemy of King Arthur, I don't suppose they would help us!"

"You are probably right," the old man answered, uncomfortable at the way Hickory said 'us'.

It was not long before the army's tents were erected, ditches dug, fires lit and guards posted. The men of d'Vert's household quickly erected his pavilion in the centre of the stone circle and before long the Green Knight and his advisors had set up their council of war.

Then, as the night fell, William d'Vert left his tent and stared out across the moor. Two bats appeared in the half-light and circled around the standing stones, but d'Vert ignored them. His mind pondered only one thought. How many warriors would join his ragged army, once the morning had come?

# 10.  Lyonesse

*~ Below the sea is a world unseen, a watery land
lost in a dream ~*

And so they came to him. From all corners of
Cornwall. To make a last valiant stand
with their liege Lord.

A handful of men-at-arms, who had escaped
the clutches of the Bretons at Restormel Castle,
were amongst the first to arrive. They followed
behind their stubborn leader, Ranulf de Roche.

He was tall and arrogant. His pointed black
beard bristled out like a challenge and as he
strode into the camp and past Fern and Hickory,
he sneered down at them, as if they were freakish
oddities left behind by a travelling circus. Ranulf
the 'rash' some called him, for he acted without
thinking and was not a knight to be trusted.

After de Roche, sixty bowmen appeared
from a scattering of villages on the edge of
Davidstow Woods. Poachers and rascals the lot
of them, but deadly accurate with the longbow
because of it!

By midday, a troop of mail-clad knights had
appeared. They had ridden down from the Green
Knight's castle at Tintagel. They spoke at length
with d'Vert and young Ethan, bringing news of
Lady Eliza and the defence of their home. When

they had eaten and rested, they joined up with the horsemen of the Company of Excalibur.

As the afternoon passed, more men came, but never enough. There were a handful of crossbowmen that had been sent from the Monastery at Bodmin. There were a hundred or so peasants and ploughmen, that came from the rich farmlands of the Vale of Mawgan. They were armed with little more than pitchforks and scythes, but they were willing to fight for their land.

Tin-miners from the far west of Cornwall, fishermen from the coastal villages, town militiamen from Helston, Redruth, St Austell and Truro all came. But they were not warriors.

As the Green Knight met the men when they arrived, he thanked them for their loyalty and their courage, but he knew that there were too few of them and that they were inexperienced in the ways of war. He would have to rely on his own men-at-arms, his loyal shield-warriors and his small band of steadfast knights. Yet at no time did the thought of asking for peace ever enter his mind. His determination was resolute. Win, or die fighting!

⚜⚜⚜

It was clear by early evening that no more men

were coming and the warriors and noblemen of the Green Knight's Court were dismayed at the thought that their army was barely two thousand strong. "It is not numbers that win battles," d'Vert reminded them, "but courage and strength of purpose!"

Then, whilst the guards began to close the camp's gates, there was one last arrival. A mail-clad knight appeared on the horizon and all eyes turned towards him as he made his way down to the entrance.

His armour was old, his sword rusty, his helmet ancient and his horse had seen better days, but there was a hidden power within his sea-blue eyes. He rode into the encampment with a noble grace and men looked upon him with a mixture of sadness and fear. As he halted and climbed down from his mount, they parted to let him through.

"Who is he?" Hickory asked Penfric, as they stood watching the newcomer arrive.

"He, young man, is Christian de Troy. The last survivor of the lost Kingdom of Lyonesse."

"Why does he have such a plain coat-of-arms?" Hickory asked, noticing that the knight's shield had no sign or symbol upon it, but just a plain blue background.

"He will have no device until he can once again display the silver swan of Lyonesse. And he will only do that when his lost land is recovered," Penfric paused, "and of course that will never be."

"Why?" asked Fern.

"Because Lyonesse has fallen beneath the waves. It is lost forever under the sea," the old jester answered.

"What is Lyonesse?" Fern was intrigued.

"What was Lyonesse, you mean," Penfric replied. "Lyonesse was a great city. A fortress of high stone towers and walls built upon the rocks on the far tip of Cornwall. A land of great beauty and a land of strong men and wise women."

"And yet it is no more?" Nathaniel, it seemed, had never heard of Lyonesse either.

"That is true. The strong men behind their tall battlements could do nothing to halt its collapse," Penfric stated.

"How did it fall?" Hickory asked.

"They say that one day the sky turned as black as the raven's wings, even though it was the middle of the afternoon. Great blasts of thunder deafened the people of Lyonesse, whilst lightning split the sky with silver splinters. Raindrops as large as a man's hand fell to the ground, the wind rose and snarled and trampled through the city like a great ravaging monster. And then it happened . . ." Penfric's eyes fell upon the boy's.

"What?" gasped Hickory.

"The sea grew," Penfric continued his tale, "it grew taller than the trees, taller than the highest towers, taller even than the mountains of Lyonesse. For a brief moment of calm, everything stopped. The rain halted, the wind dropped to a soft breath, even the thunder and lightning stopped in awe of the sea. The people in the streets of the cities stood still, the farmers in the fields dropped their tools, the merchants and the traders on the quays looked far out to the blue horizon and everything was silent."

"And?" Hickory tugged at the old jester's tunic.

"A wave came. A wave so powerful, that it shook the very foundations of the city. A wave larger than anything ever seen. And it rose and then fell upon Lyonesse like a hungry dragon."

"So how did he escape?" Fern whispered as she watched Christian de Troy unsaddle his grey horse.

"He was just a boy, when it happened. His father saw the waves coming first, as he strolled the ramparts of the great city. He ran to find his son and put him on the fastest steed in the kingdom. He kissed the boy's forehead and struck the horse's behind. The boy rode and rode with the great wave following him like a snarling beast. But he did not stop. Nor did he even turn to look back, until the wave had died behind him, and he had reached safety." Penfric halted for a moment and his face looked sad.

"But, when he did look back, the sight broke the lad's heart. For there was nothing there except the wide, wide ocean. In the distance he could see the tops of the mountains, a few outcrops of land where there had once been a whole kingdom. A land where men had farmed, women had sung and children had played. And now it was all lost beneath the waves."

"No wonder he looks so forlorn," Fern murmured.

"There is only one thing that de Troy took with him," Penfric added.

"What?" Fern whispered.

"Watch," Penfric pointed toward the knight, as he stroked his horse and spoke quietly to it in a strange tongue.

"He is speaking to the horse in Lyonet, the ancient language of the city beneath the sea. You see, that horse is the one that carried Christian to safety; it is his best friend and his last remaining link to his homeland and his family."

Fern felt tears running down her face. She licked her lips and felt the salt taste of her tears. Whether she cried for the sad knight or for her own loss she didn't know, but she knew that Christian de Troy would be her friend.

# 11. Dragonboy

*~ Look behind the face and find a heart of grace ~*

"Watch," Fern pointed out into the growing darkness as Hickory followed her finger to a patch of trees on the edge of the moor.

"Here he comes." They both watched carefully as a small figure emerged from the branches and zig-zagged across the open moorland. There he stopped and suddenly rolled to the floor and slipped under the tent at the far end of the encampment.

Fern and Hickory waited and moments later, the small figure re-appeared clutching a sack. After taking a quick glance around, he darted back over the moor like a fox.

"Let's follow him," said Hickory and as dusk fell, both of them pursued the small figure across the heath-land.

The shape moved quickly and the darkness of the night seemed not to hinder his speed at all. Fern and Hickory were also at home in the open and they had little trouble following the figure as he made his way across the moor.

After about two miles, the small shape suddenly halted. Fern and Hickory dived behind an outcrop of stone and watched to see what the figure was going to do next.

Peering around the rock, the children saw that the shape was a small boy. He had stopped because his stolen sack had got caught up in a tangle of branches from a fallen tree.

After a few moments of pulling and tugging, the sack ripped open and the contents spilled out. The boy cried out in anger and tried to scoop up the fallen flour, but it was an impossible task.

Fern and Hickory nodded to each other and then stepped out into the open. The lad's hearing was good and even though the children moved with the deftness of deer, the boy turned to face them.

As he stared at the children and they gazed upon him, all three of them gasped at the faces they saw before them.

The boy blinked his eyes in disbelief. The last thing he had expected to see behind him were two green children. He backed away from them, forgetting all about the bag of flour that lay ruined on the ground.

Yet, the green children also found that they too, were recoiling away from the young boy. They had never come across anything like him in all their wanderings.

Standing there in the darkness, staring at each other, with their mouths agape, all three children suddenly broke out into laughter.

"Are you piskies?" the boy enquired as he took a tentative step toward Fern and Hickory.

"No," Fern answered. She'd heard Penfric tell stories of the Cornish fairy-folk. "We are the same as you, it's just our skin colour that is different."

"I hope you're not the same as me," the boy replied with bitterness.

"What do you mean?" Hickory asked.

"I saw how you looked upon me," the lad sat down upon a clump of grass.

"No different to how you looked at us!" Hickory sat down next to him.

"Don't come too close," the boy inched away from Hickory.

"I won't harm you," Hickory smiled.

"But, I might bring harm to you!" the lad declared.

The children were dismayed that they could not bring comfort to the boy. It was true; his face had given them a shock at first. It seemed as if the poor child had been burnt in a fire or trampled on by wild horses, it was so badly disfigured. But Fern and Hickory had learnt to look beyond such things as outward appearances.

"What happened to you?" Fern sat down on the other side of the boy, and took his hand in hers.

"I have leprosy," the boy replied, snatching

his hand from hers.

Fern and Hickory looked to each other for help, but neither of them had heard of the disease.

The boy was sharp and he saw their fleeting glance. "You don't know what that is do you?" He stood up and made to leave.

"Wait," Fern pleaded, "tell us. Perhaps, we can help."

The boy laughed. "No one can do anything. Not even piskies!"

"Please," continued Fern, "tell us anyway."

"Here," Hickory drew something from his tunic, "it's a piece of waybread." He had made a habit of keeping some morsel of food about his person, ever since they had nearly starved in the snow near Lincoln.

The boy himself was clearly hungry and he could not resist the bread. He took it from Hickory's grasp and sat back down, though well away from the children.

He tore into the bread and munched away noisily. His disfigured nose was wide and flat and his nostrils were squashed, which meant he made a loud gurgling kind of sound when he ate.

After a few mouthfuls he smiled and his twisted mouth did its best to smile. "My name is Toby," he muttered before munching again, "though people tend to call me Gebbedy."

"What does that mean?" Fern was pleased

to see the boy beginning to trust them.

"It's Cornish," the lad replied. "It means dragon boy."

Gebbedy looked pleased with his nickname, though in truth the people of his village had shouted it at him as an insult, before they drove him and his mother out of Treviscoe.

"Well, Gebbedy," Fern stood up, "I'm Fern and this is my brother Hickory." Hickory stood up too and bowed in front of the boy.

Gebbedy smiled and then continued to eat. In a couple of mouthfuls he finished the waybread and then he too jumped up. "Time to leave," he stated, "Mother, will begin to worry!"

"Where do you live, Gebbedy?" Fern wanted to help the boy further.

"I'll show you, if you can keep up with me," Gebbedy answered and then, quick as a jack-rabbit he bounced up a mound of scree and was away again, across the moor. Hickory and Fern took up the challenge and for another mile or two they ran after the boy.

Every now and then, Gebbedy looked back to see if he had lost them, but they were still following behind him. He laughed when he spotted them. It was if they were playing some giant game of tag, right across Bodmin moor.

Eventually, Gebbedy slowed down and then, by a rocky outcrop near Garrow Tor, he halted and turned to meet his pursuers.

"You must come no closer," Gebbedy insisted, as Fern and Hickory caught up with him.

"Why not?" Fern gasped, catching her breath.

"Because no-one is allowed inside the colony, unless they too are a leper!" Gebbedy spoke sadly and then he pointed to a cluster of ragged stone houses and wooden huts.

Through the mists and darkness, the children followed his finger and stared at the dead village before them. It was like staring into a nightmare.

They saw figures dressed in rags, faces covered, working away in the dark night. Half-starved, skeletal figures that drifted across this desolate patch of moor land, like ghostly phantoms.

"We come out at night," Gebbedy explained. "It's harder for people to see us in the dark and in truth, the less we see of each other, the less we have to think about our own plight."

Fern had never seen anything so desperate. It was worse even than the plague-ridden streets of Lincoln. She drew her gaze away from the dismal scene and sat down in thought.

"Is there no cure?" Hickory gasped as he caught sight of a man chopping wood. The moon had shone on the blade of his axe and the man's ravaged face loomed out of the blackness like a ghoul.

"No," Gebbedy answered solemnly, "so, leave us alone and return back to your soldier camp." With that, the boy took one last look at the two green children and then before Fern or Hickory could speak again, he scampered back into the colony.

Would his mother believe he had met piskies, Gebbedy thought, as he opened the door of their hut? Doubt it! But she will wonder why I've returned empty-handed, with half of Cornwall sitting in tents on Bodmin Moor!

## 12. Knights and Lepers
### ~ *The dead do tell tales!* ~

"**H**is Lordship would see you, urgently!" Christian de Troy spoke softly as he entered the children's tent.

"Why?" asked Fern, who was deep in conversation with Nathaniel.

"He knows of your healing powers," de Troy replied.

All night, Fern, Hickory and Nathaniel had discussed ways of helping Gebbedy and the leper colony. It hadn't occurred to her that it would be of any concern to the great warriors that surrounded her in this camp. So what did d'Vert really want?

Hurriedly, they all filed out into the spring sunshine and walked across the encampment, toward the Green Knight's pavilion.

"Hickory tells me you can cure these poor wretches," d'Vert stared at the green girl before him.

"Possibly," Fern stated defiantly. She turned and glared at her brother. "Why has nothing been done for them before now?" she asked.

"My hands are tied in such matters," d'Vert stated, "according to the Church, they are already dead. The law doesn't recognise them either."

"That's right, I'm afraid," added Christian de Troy. "If a husband catches leprosy then his wife has to choose whether to follow him to the colony, or accept that she is now a widow. It is a harsh rule!"

"You are too soft, de Troy!" Ranulf de Roche interrupted. "These wretches will spread their filthy disease to all and sundry if they are not kept away from the rest of us."

"So, why are you so keen to help, them now?" Fern stared back at the Green Knight.

"Because, my dear, they are Cornish, they are my people and I would help them, if I could. Yet I am not a healer, nor do I possess a Merlin who can weave wizardry. But you, I understand, do have such powers!" he replied.

Fern was trapped! She desperately wanted to help Gebbedy and the lepers, but she was not sure as to the motives behind d'Vert's sudden interest. She glanced at Hickory, but he was too busy fetching the Green Knight a goblet of wine. It was Nathaniel who saw the anxiety in her eyes, but he had no answer for her either.

Fern looked to the floor of the tent and closed her eyes briefly. Then, she looked back at

the knights before her. "Yes," she replied, "I believe I can help the lepers!"


Although the barren landscape of Bodmin moor was an easy place to get lost upon, it was not difficult for Hickory to follow their trail from last night and with his instinctive tracking skills, the small band of riders found themselves on the outskirts of the leper colony within the hour.

As they approached the settlement, they stopped by a rough stone table that stood at the entrance and stared down at a wooden bowl that sat upon it. A ray of sunlight streamed down through the grey skies and Fern saw something glint within the bowl. She bent down to get a closer look and saw a handful of silver coins lying in some liquid.

"It's vinegar, I expect," said Nathaniel answering Fern's inquisitiveness. "The belief is that the acid properties of the vinegar will destroy any leprosy. The coins have been left here by the lepers to pay those that bring them food."

"That's right," Penfric added, "they call it the Devil's punchbowl!"

Entering the colony, the riders started to hang back. Even Nathaniel slowed his pace, but Fern and Hickory strode purposefully forward.

"They are fearless," Christian de Troy stated with admiration, as the children dismounted from their horses.

"They are foolish," remarked Ranulf de Roche, who now held a scarf to his mouth, and refused to take a step closer.

There was no sign of the lepers. Smoke funnelled from a handful of the stone houses and a few stray chickens clucked and squawked, but not one single soul could be seen.

"Gebbedy!" Hickory shouted.

"We've come to help you!" Fern called out.

Then, very slowly, the earth around them seemed to move. Ragged ghosts arose from the moors, shadows of men, women and children. The horses reared up and some of the riders drew back.

"Foul creatures! What use are they to anyone?" Ranulf de Roche muttered, reining his horse back as the leper colony stood before them.

"You know why we are here, de Roche," the Green Knight rebuked him. "Let's just see what the girl can do."

"Can she perform miracles, my Lord? They are dead to us, look at them! They are disgusting, their limbs would break at the touch of a feather and if they were to march into battle, the best we could hope for is that they might scare the Bretons back to Brittany."

"Quiet, de Roche. I don't yet know if they can be of any use to us, but I do know that the girl won't help them if she suspects my plans. She does not believe in this war." William d'Vert turned his horse to meet the lepers with a smile.

"What do you want?" A tall woman stepped forward from the colony and approached them. Her face was shrouded and only her eyes could be seen, but her voice was clear and crisp.

"We want to help you," Fern answered. "We want to try and heal you."

At this remark, many of the lepers laughed. A number of them began to go back to their duties, but some looked upon the green girl with hope.

"How can you help us?" The woman stared at Fern with a mixture of fear and unease. "What are you anyway?"

Nathaniel then dismounted from Windwalker, and strode over to Fern. He took her hand in his and addressed the lepers, "This girl," he stated calmly, "this girl is from the wilds and she has a way with herbs and plants the like of which I have never seen before. She helped cure the plague in Lincoln, she has nursed children back from the brink of death and now she says she can help you. Do you not at least have the courage to try?"

The lepers grew silent, some returned to listen to the strangers again and suddenly from the back of the colony, a little figure ran forward. It was Gebbedy!

"I would be cured!" he grinned. "You can heal me."

"Gebbedy!" The tall woman called to the boy. "Don't you dare!"

"But, Mother," he replied, "these are the piskies I met last night." The crowds, both knights and lepers, laughed at this, although some from each side stared at the green children with similar thoughts in their heads.

Gebbedy was not to be deterred and he tugged Fern's hands. "I am ready to become Toby again," he pleaded.

Fern crossed to her horse, Moon-Shadow, and reached up for her pack. She pulled it free and returned to the centre of the colony, as all eyes watched her.

She dug deep and pulled out various bags full of herbal extracts and the like. Hickory brought over a pot that he'd taken from one of the huts and then they both moved toward the small fire that sat whistling and spitting by Gebbedy's stone shack.

Everyone stared at Fern whilst she measured out different amounts of her remedy. Then, she poured them into the boiling water and stirred the mixture carefully.

Steam rose from the cooking pot, the crowd

mumbled and muttered and Gebbedy stared at the flames. Fern picked up a bowl and slowly ladled some of the potion into it. After blowing upon it to help it to cool, she took a tiny sip.

After judging it to be about right, she motioned Gebbedy forward. The boy's mother was anxious, but at the same time intrigued, so she let her boy take the medicine.

Gebbedy took a big gulp of Fern's remedy and wiped his chin.

"Well?" one of the lepers shouted, as they drew closer to the boy.

"Well, it's hot!" laughed Gebbedy.

"You must wait," Fern answered the questioning stares.

The Green Knight and his entourage started to talk and the lepers sat down upon the floor of their settlement. It was almost an hour before Gebbedy felt anything.

"Look!" his mother cried. "Look at Gebbedy's face!"

A grey shadow seemed to have been lifted from the boy's face. The sores, which had been open and weeping, were now starting to heal, and in places they had disappeared altogether. The boy stood up for all to see what his mother was now pointing at. Then, he ran to her, and wrapped his arms around her waist.

His nose was still flat and his scars would

remain, but his face was already pink with health and his mouth beamed with a crooked smile.

"No more night-walking, for you," she said, ruffling Gebbedy's hair. Then, she turned to the rest of the colony.

Fighting back tears, she spoke, "This girl seems to have cured my son, I will let her try with me too."

"And me," another leper shouted.

"Me too!" cried another.

It was not long before Nathaniel and Hickory had formed the lepers into orderly queues and Fern began administering her cure to the whole colony. And within a few hours, a sound rang out through the desolate settlement of huts and shacks that had not been heard there for a long time. Laughter, healthy laughter!

By late afternoon, they were done. Every man, woman and child in the colony had been cured. They would always have scars to remind them of their suffering, but the grey shadows that had lain upon their faces had been lifted. Their sores and lesions were already beginning to heal, too. And though many would never be as they once were, all would be able to return to their homes. Fern had brought them back to life, in sight of the church and the law, at least!

"Now, we have cured you," d'Vert stated proudly.

"What does he mean, we?" Fern mumbled, whilst d'Vert addressed the colony.

"We ask only one favour in return."

"What's he up to?" Nathaniel whispered.

"I need you to show your loyalty to me. I need you to show your loyalty to Cornwall," d'Vert, paused for a moment, "I need men!"

Fern's face flushed with anger and she turned upon the Green Knight with fury. "I didn't cure them so they could join your war. I didn't bring them back from the dead, only to fall in battle!"

"I have barely two thousand soldiers under my command, young lady. I need every healthy man to help defend Cornwall. You have made these men fit. You have given me warriors." It was d'Vert who was growing angry now. "Besides, if they do not fight, if we do not win, then, there will be no Cornwall for them to live in anyway!"

With that, d'Vert rode toward the crowd and behind him, Ranulf de Roche and the rest of the knights began to cheer.

Tentatively, the men of the leper colony came forward to listen further to their Lord's words.

Fern and Nathaniel backed away from the scene.

"I am sorry, Fern," young Ethan d'Vert

walked toward her and apologised for his father's conduct. "I am afraid he will stop at nothing to defend this land."

"So I see," Fern answered him and then she turned her back upon the colony, as a hundred, now healthy men, eagerly lined up to join the Green Knight's army!

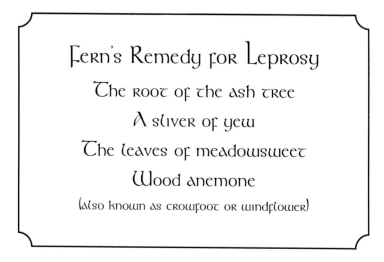

Fern's Remedy for Leprosy

The root of the ash tree

A sliver of yew

The leaves of meadowsweet

Wood anemone

(also known as crowfoot or windflower)

# 13. Squire Hickory

*~ With the touch of the blade, a knight is made~*

It was late. The sun had dipped below the moor hours ago, but candles still burned in the pavilion of the Green Knight.

In the corner of the court, a small figure dressed in a green surcoat, dozed upon a three-legged stool. Helping his sister cure the lepers that afternoon, had worn him out. All around him, the council of war debated and argued the best way to defeat the Breton army and then, drawing away from the discussion, Sir William spotted his standard bearer, half-asleep.

"I need a new squire, young man," he called across the tent. "Mine will soon be moving up." The nobles fell silent as he addressed Hickory. And all eyes turned to the youngster. Hickory awoke with a start and jumped up from his stool, his face beaming with pride.

"What say you?" D'Vert asked.

Do not be too hasty, lad, Nathaniel thought to himself and from the far side of the tent, he looked past the knights and nobles, and wished with all his might that Hickory would say no.

Yet, he knew the boy had been bewitched by the grandeur and the chivalry of the Green Knight's court and his answer came as no surprise to the old man.

"Yes, my Lord. It would be a great honour."

The knights cheered and patted the boy's back, while Nathaniel bit his tongue and thought about how he would break the news to Fern.

"Then, in the morning, you shall attend on me," d'Vert continued. "Now Ethan, away to the priest and prepare yourself!"

"Yes, Father," Ethan d'Vert rose from his own stool next to Hickory, and moved to the doorway of the great tent.

"What must you prepare for?" Hickory asked him as he lifted the flap.

"Well, now you are his squire, I have a new rank."

"What is it?" Hickory asked.

"Wait and see," Ethan replied, as he slipped away to find the priest.

"Today's the day, then!" Nathaniel stated as he wrapped a cloak around himself and prepared for the early morning chill.

"What do you mean?" asked Hickory rising from his bed.

"Today, our young friend Ethan becomes a knight."

"So that's what he meant," Hickory thought

back to the evening before.

"Hadn't you noticed that he has not eaten for twenty-four hours?"

"I saw that he drank only water last night," Hickory replied.

"He has fasted and he would have spent all last night with the priest in prayer. This morning he will bathe and then he will be pure of body and mind," Nathaniel stated knowledgeably. "In less than an hour the ceremony will begin."

"Can we watch?" Hickory's voice could not hide his excitement.

"I should think so, Hickory," the old man grinned. "After all, you are the Green Knight's squire and you are an important part of the service."

"Really?" The boy's face glowed with enthusiasm. "This is all like being in one of your tales about ancient warriors."

"Perhaps," replied Nathaniel, "but we must not forget our own quest."

"Can Fern watch too?" Hickory asked, whilst he buttoned up his surcoat and stroked the emblem of the golden tree upon his chest.

"I should think so, although I don't suppose she will be very interested, do you? Where is your sister, anyway?" Nathaniel glanced at the empty bed in the corner of the tent.

"She wanders the moors to watch the sun

rise each morning," Hickory answered. "Haven't you noticed? Oh no of course not, you're never awake early enough!" he continued.

"A privilege of age, young man!" the old man retorted with a smile. "Now let's find some breakfast. I'm sure I can smell bacon." And with that Nathaniel lifted the tent flap and the two of them greeted the new day.

❦❦❦

A trumpet called out across the moor and at that signal young Ethan d'Vert, robed in a pure white tunic, was led across the camp to his father's great pavilion.

The whole camp had turned out to see the knighthood ceremony, for the Green Knight had hoped to make it an event that would galvanise his army, bringing them together as one. So, as Ethan marched proudly forward, the crowds cheered. At the entrance of the tent, the Company of Excalibur stood tall and raised their swords as the heir to the Duchy of Cornwall passed under them.

Inside the pavilion, Ethan was greeted by a host of candles that flickered and lit the interior, like the stars on a dark night. People had crammed themselves all along the sides of the tent and they all fell silent as Ethan entered.

Nathaniel and Fern were in amongst the assembled knights and noblemen and Christian de Troy stood nearby, too.

But young Ethan only had eyes for those in front of him. At the centre of this small group was his father, William d'Vert. Next to him was the priest, robed in black and on the other side of the Green Knight stood Hickory, holding high the Green Knight's Standard.

As the pavilion grew silent, William d'Vert spoke solemnly, "Today, this young man becomes a knight. Today he vows loyal service to his God and to his Lord."

The assembly dutifully applauded as Ethan walked forward, head bowed, to stand before his father. The priest now moved into the centre of the tent and d'Vert passed him the shining sword that sat upon the table.

"Ethan d'Vert," the priest's deep voice echoed through the crowded pavilion, "this sword represents justice and loyalty. Use it to defend the church and all servants of God!" He passed the sword to Ethan and the young warrior pushed the blade into his belt. "Do you promise to follow the code of chivalry?" the priest continued.

"I do," declared Ethan.

William d'Vert now moved forward and took his own sword from its scabbard. "Kneel down before me," he spoke solemnly to his son and

Ethan bent low before him.

Then, d'Vert tapped him lightly on both shoulders and spoke again, "In the name of God and Saint Patrin, I dub thee a Knight. Arise, Sir Ethan."

The young knight stood up and the surrounding nobles and priests all clapped. Outside, the soldiers cheered and music began playing.

And so it was, that young Ethan d'Vert became a knight, and Hickory, holding the Standard straight throughout the ceremony, found himself squire to William d'Vert.

# The Code of Chivalry

Justice: seek always the path of right

Loyalty: sworn by oath to defend your Lord

Courage: to fight until the death

Humility: never boast of your triumphs

Prowess: to seek excellence in everything

# 14. The Tournament
## ~ Take borage for courage ~

The feast to celebrate the knighthood ceremony was meagre and certainly not what it would have been, had it taken place at Tintagel Castle. But an army in the field had to take what it found, and the men were pleased enough to have hot stew and warm bread in their bellies.

After the feast, some of the knights and ladies danced whilst Penfric played the shawm. The children sang and the men toasted their new knight.

Then, William d'Vert stood up, and his voice resounded over the lines of trestle tables before him. "I require a leader for our vanguard of knights. A Captain for the Company of Excalibur." His eyes searched the faces of the noblemen before him. "It is a job for a brave and valiant man, one who others will follow, one who is prepared to lead his men to death and glory!"

"I will lead the men, if they will have me!" Christian de Troy arose up from his place between Fern and Nathaniel, and the noblemen cheered.

"Excellent!" d'Vert stated. "But is there no-one else prepared to take on such an honour? No-one to challenge de Troy?" It was clear the Green

Knight wanted competition, he wanted his men hungry to lead and desperate to fight.

"I'll lead them!" Ranulf de Roche threw his gauntlet down on the grass in front of Christian de Troy and stared at him defiantly. "I'll do a better job than this boy!"

"I am no boy!" de Troy replied calmly. "I am the last man of Lyonesse and it would be an honour to defend Cornwall as such."

"An honour, my backside!" roared de Roche.

"You just want fame and glory. Perhaps you hope to earn a device for that plain shield of yours?" Ranulf smirked.

"Maybe we could design something appropriate for you," de Roche sniggered. "A clump of seaweed perhaps, that seems to represent your homeland well. At least what's left of it!"

Ranulf's men laughed but the rest of the nobles were grim-faced. Fern and Hickory's cheeks burned red with anger and even Nathaniel looked irritated, but Christian de Troy remained as placid as the sea on a windless day.

"That's enough de Roche!" The Green Knight restored order.

"Just playing with the fellow, my Lord," de Roche replied as he picked up his gauntlet.

"So you also wish to lead the Company?" the Green Knight stared at him.

"Yes," de Roche replied with a grin.

"Wonderful!" exclaimed d'Vert. "A challenge indeed!" d'Vert was pleased, he wanted to set the men's minds hard upon the battle ahead and a contest of arms was a good way to do it.

"Now, sword, mace or lance? That is the question," d'Vert thought aloud. "Well, as it is to lead cavalry, then I think by lance would be most appropriate."

"Excellent idea!" de Roche laughed, his reputation as a jousting champion was well documented.

"Your challenge is accepted," Christian quietly replied.

"A joust to celebrate my son's coming of age then. What could be better?" d'Vert was beaming! He turned and signalled to his attendants, "Set up the lists!"

"These are the rules," proclaimed Penfric, who had been made herald for the occasion. "There will be three jousts. If you break your lance on your opponent's chest you gain one point. If you break it on his helmet, you gain two points. And if you unhorse your opponent, you gain three points. The winner will become the Captain of the Company of Excalibur."

Christian de Troy and Ranulf de Roche faced each other and nodded their agreement to the rules. Then, a squire brought forth a silver tray. Upon it were two goblets of wine. The squire handed one to de Roche and the other to de Troy. Both men toasted the Green Knight, and downed their drinks. After replacing their goblets on the tray, they walked toward their mounts and prepared for the first joust.

At one end, Ranulf de Roche took the reins of his horse from his squire and checked his spurs. He was a powerfully built man, and crammed into his armour he looked like a huge black bull. After mounting his horse, he drew down the visor of his helmet and then his squire handed him his shield. It was polished black, just like his armour, but in the centre of it was the de Roche coat-of-arms - a white dragon.

At the other end of the lists, Christian de Troy also prepared himself. His shield was plain blue, his armour did not shine and he was not as muscular as de Roche, but there was something about him that resonated inner strength.

As the two men turned to face each other, the crowds on either side of the lists now grew silent. They couched their lances under their arms. The Green Knight dropped his hand to signal the start of the first joust, the trumpet blew and the horses charged!

Such was the speed of the first encounter, that Hickory, sitting at the Green Knight's side, almost missed it! He had never seen such a spectacle before and was amazed when neither de Roche nor de Troy were hit on their first attempt. Instead, both knights charged passed each other, their lances narrowly missing their intended targets.

"That was mighty close!" Ethan d'Vert whispered to Hickory, as the two knights prepared for the second joust.

"Yes," said Hickory, still dazzled by the whole event, "I wish I could have a go."

The Green Knight laughed at this and turned to him. "Now you're a squire, you are on the ladder to knighthood, young man. So who knows, one day, you might just get that wish!" Hickory beamed, but on the far side of the lists, far away from the Green Knight's entourage, Fern and Nathaniel had spotted something amiss.

"Look," Fern pointed toward Christian de Troy. "There's something wrong!"

She was right! For as de Troy lent over to take his second lance from his squire, he shook in his saddle. The squire had to hold his horse steady as de Troy couched the new lance and turned to face de Roche again.

The trumpet sounded and the two knights charged for the second time. Yet, Christian de Troy was struggling to stay in his saddle, a great tiredness had come upon him like some huge wave. Then, his eyes seemed to close and the lance loosened in his grip. Just before impact, it slipped from his grasp completely and fell harmlessly to the floor. Seconds later, Ranulf de Roche's lance smashed into de Troy's face, and shattered into hundreds of wooden shards.

Somehow, Christian kept his balance and carried on riding through to the end of the tilt, but it was clear that he was in trouble. As he dismounted, he fell to the ground and his squire ran to assist him. At the other end, hidden behind the cover of his helmet, Ranulf de Roche grinned, broadly!

"Quarter, my Lord!" Ethan asked his father, as he ran to check on de Troy.

"What?" demanded de Roche, removing his helmet and watching proudly as two points were awarded to him on the scoring board.

"Quarter, I beg time for Christian to regain his composure," Ethan continued.

"You have five minutes!" the Green Knight answered.

"Father, please! That is not enough time," Ethan pleaded with him.

"Five minutes," d'Vert repeated, and then turned to watch Penfric juggle.

De Roche smiled knowingly. There was no way de Troy would be ready in five minutes! The captaincy of the Company of Excalibur was as good as his!

"He's been drugged!" Nathaniel rose from the slumped body of Christian de Troy and stared at the figures inside de Troy's tent.

"What do you mean?" Ethan knelt down to check de Troy himself.

"I mean he's been drugged. Clearly, Ranulf de Roche is very keen to lead your father's men!"

"I do not have the herbs that can revive him in five minutes," Fern added.

"Then he has lost his chance to lead us!" Ethan looked downcast. He knew the men did not want de Roche to command them. It would have a disastrous effect on morale. And they needed all the faith they could muster if they had any hope against the Bretons.

"Someone must take his place," Nathaniel mumbled half to himself.

"That's it!" Ethan started to take off de Troy's armour.

"Not you, Ethan," Nathaniel added, "you will be missed."

For a moment all went silent in the tent and then Fern grabbed hold of de Troy's shield. "I will take his place!" she said calmly.

"But you don't care if he wins or loses!" Hickory was outraged at this suggestion.

"Christian is my friend," she answered,

"and although I don't agree with this war, I also understand why he wants to lead the knights. His pride and his honour is all that he has left."

"But you must score three points to win Fern. That means knocking de Roche off his horse!" Ethan stared at her with doubt in his eyes.

"I will do the best I can," Fern replied. "There is more to me than what you see before you!"

"Let her try," Nathaniel stated calmly. He knew the girl well enough to realise when she meant business.

So, they quickly dressed her in the chain-mail hauberk, the coif, the gauntlets and de Troy's blue surcoat. Finally, the great helmet was placed upon her head.

"Well, you look the part," Nathaniel stood back and stared at Fern. "Thank God the helmet and the armour fit."

"You can see why we wear our coat-of-arms on our tunics," Ethan stated as Fern stood before them. "Once you have a helmet on, no one can tell who you are. In the midst of battle, you could end up slaughtering your own side!"

Even Hickory had to agree that his sister, hidden under de Troy's armour, could just about pass as the Knight from Lyonesse.

"Now for the lance," Nathaniel said as he

handed it to Fern.

"I can barely hold it, let alone fight with it," she cried, dropping the weapon to the floor. "It's far too heavy!"

"Let me do it, then," Hickory protested, "I've practised at the quintain at least. She's never even held a sword, let alone a lance. Besides she hates fighting!"

"No," Nathaniel replied, "like Ethan you will be required to sit next to his Lordship, only Fern won't be missed."

"Anyway," Fern added, "I'm tall enough to get away with the deception."

"No use being tall enough, if you can't hold a lance!" Hickory smirked in reply.

"I have an idea," Nathaniel said, looking over to the back of the tent. They followed his gaze and their eyes fell upon the staves that held the small pavilion up.

"Quick, get one of those over here," he stated.

Hickory ran over and pulled a stave free, then, grudgingly, he handed it to his sister.

"Perfect," said Fern, "it's made of willow which means it's tough and shock-resistant, but very light." She spoke knowledgably and then easily lifted the new lance up.

"Quick, tie one of these blue ribbons around the end," Ethan cried. "And let's hope no-one looks at it too carefully."

Moments later, Fern dressed in the armour and surcoat of Christian de Troy, left the tent to a chorus of cheers.

"Ready to resume, de Troy?" the Green Knight bellowed from his platform, as Ethan and Hickory re- joined him.

Fern nodded, glad that the deception seemed to be working and then she strode over to de Troy's steed.

The squire that held the horse knew that something was wrong, but he did not give Fern away. Like most of the men in the encampment, he wanted de Troy to win. He held out the reins to Fern and she took them confidently.

If anyone else had tried to mount the grey horse from Lyonesse, other than de Troy, there would have been a problem, but Fern gently whispered in the steed's ear and mounted it with ease. Then, she pulled on the reins, turned it around and prepared to charge.

At the other end of the lists, Ranulf de Roche sat upon his horse, dumbfounded. He had not expected to see de Troy again that day, presuming that the potion would have knocked him for six! He lifted his visor and glared at his squire who had mixed the concoction for him. The man held up his hands in bafflement, and backed away, fearful of de Roche's anger.

Then, from the Green Knight's stand, a trumpet called and Fern hurriedly grabbed a handful of herbs from her saddlebag and threw them into her mouth. Chewing them down, she prayed that the borage leaves would give her the courage that she needed.

Ranulf de Roche now realised that he would have to engage in the final joust. Yet the thought did not worry him, for surely de Troy would still be suffering from the drugged wine. So he made his way to the lists, faced down and couched his lance for the last run. He shouted an insult and then his black steed's nostrils snorted and its front legs rose into the air. Then, they pounded down on the ground like a crack of thunder and he charged.

"So the healer fights," Nathaniel whispered under his breath, as Fern and de Roche hurtled toward each other.

As Fern rode down the lists she seemed to become as one with the horse and the lance, interlocking in a single, symmetrical movement. The crowd of experienced soldiers and knights had never seen anything like it before and even the Green Knight was impressed with the way 'de Troy' moved.

As for Fern herself, she was amazed with the natural thrill that surged through her body as she charged down the lists. It was the power of nature that coursed through her, and nature, though at times gentle and caring, could also unleash terrible wrath.

All eyes now turned to watch the outcome of the final joust, though Hickory and Ethan d'Vert could hardly bear to watch. Closer and closer the two knights came now, bearing down upon each other at great speed. Hooves pounded, bodies tightened and the crowd drew their breath. Then, at the moment of collision, both Fern and de Roche thrust forward their lances and aimed for their opponent.

It was Ranulf de Roche who took the initiative and his lance was thrust first, but Fern had spotted his manoeuvre and arching her head backwards, de Roche's lance narrowly missed her face. At the same time she twisted away from his attack and somehow managed to shove her willow lance upward and into de Roche's shoulder.

The weight of Fern's strike would not normally have bothered de Roche, but because she had used the momentum of her horse's strength the lance hit him with immense power.

Giving out a resounding cry, Ranulf de Roche suddenly found himself flying backwards

off his steed and landing on his back in the mud!

A great shout of approval rang out through the moorland camp and through the narrow eye-slit of her helmet, Fern smiled as she saw three points put up, next to de Troy's banner.

But de Roche wasn't finished. Lying in the dirt, his anger rose and as his squire pulled him to his feet, he took his mace from his belt. He held the weapon high above his head and then he charged at Fern, who was dismounting from her horse.

"Look out!" Hickory screamed at his sister. But Fern did not need the warning, she felt de Roche coming, her instincts had told her and as he came upon her the crowd gasped. But Fern ducked away from de Roche's strike and rolled onto the ground, just in time. Ranulf turned to strike again, but before he could, he found the brawny arms of a number of knights wrestling him to the ground.

Then more knights swarmed toward Fern, they raised her up high onto their shoulders and the crowd applauded. She made sure she held on tight to her helmet, just to ensure the deception was not discovered. Then there was a loud chorus of cheers for Christian de Troy, the Captain of the Company of Excalibur. Though it was not actually loud enough to wake the real Christian de Troy, who lay fast asleep, inside his tent!

# Rules of the Noble Joust

Unhorse your opponent for three points

Break a lance on his helmet for two points

Break a lance on his chest for one point

⟡⟡⟡⟡⟡⟡

*The winning knight will lead the*
*Company of Excalibur.*

# 15. Storm-rider
*~A sword's strength lies not in the steel~*

By the time de Troy had finally awoken, news had spread throughout the camp that the Breton army had marched all day, and had now made base, barely two miles away. So, after hearing of Fern's exploits and laughing along with the others, de Troy soon made himself busy preparing for the coming battle.

"It will be tomorrow," he told Hickory, whilst he polished his sword and oiled his armour.

"What will?" Hickory replied.

"The battle with the Bretons. The Green Knight will lead us up to Camlann Ridge in the morning, and there we will make our stand."

"Will we win?" Hickory asked, hesitantly.

"I don't know, Hickory. We are heavily outnumbered, but we will have the high ground and we are fighting for our homeland. That will make our soldiers fight twice as hard."

He carried on cleaning his armour and then a guard suddenly rushed over to the two of them, and whispered something into de Troy's ear. Christian looked up and glanced over at an empty patch of ground at the far side of the camp. Then he excused himself, and made his way purposefully toward the Green Knight's great pavilion.

Hickory watched him as he spoke briefly to Penfric and then disappeared inside the tent.

"My Lord," Christian de Troy approached the Green Knight, who was warming himself by the fire, "Ranulf de Roche and his men have left."

"What do you mean, left?" William d'Vert's voice rose in pitch.

"The guards at the west gate said that he and his men struck their tents and rode away barely fifteen minutes ago!"

"Damn the man!" d'Vert threw his goblet of wine to the floor. "We must keep this news to ourselves," he continued. "It will unsettle the men."

"Yes, my Lord," de Troy replied.

"He'll ride to him, won't he?" d'Vert asked aloud.

"Yes, my Lord. I imagine that he has already entered the Breton camp and given his loyalty to Robert Guiscard." Christian de Troy's face looked downcast.

"Then he can have him!" The Green Knight strode across the pavilion and poured himself another goblet of wine. "But I will look for de Roche on the field of battle tomorrow, Christian. You can be sure of that!"

❦❦❦

"Look what the Green Knight has given me!" Hickory bounded over to Nathaniel and Fern, who were sat outside their tent, watching the wind chase the clouds.

"What is it?" Nathaniel asked.

"It's my sword," said Hickory excitedly, as he unwrapped his gift from the scarlet cloth that it was bound up in.

"Is that all?" huffed Fern and she rose from the ground and marched back inside the tent, closed the flap and went to bed.

Nathaniel frowned, he knew Fern was unhappy that they were still here in the midst of war, but what could he do? Hickory was honour-bound to d'Vert and they were on the brink of battle. He had to stand with the boy, if only to protect him in the coming onslaught.

"Sit down lad, and show me then." Hickory ignored his sister's exit and sat down with the old man and passed over his new sword. Nathaniel handled the weapon and felt its weight in his hands. He swung it to and fro and then carefully studied its blade. "Not bad," he stated, "not bad at all. What's it called?" he asked as he handed it back to Hickory.

Hickory looked perplexed, "It doesn't have a name, Nat, it's just a sword!"

"No lad, it's much more than that. Tomorrow, in the horror of battle, it's all that stands between you and a Breton warrior's death charge. This sword is your new best friend and if you are taking it into battle with you tomorrow, then it needs a name."

"Does your sword have a name then?" Hickory smirked, knowing that Nathaniel did not carry a weapon.

But the old man stood up and walked quietly into the tent. Hickory looked on and then he appeared back again and unrolled his old grey cloak. Hickory watched as Nathaniel bent down and picked up an old leather scabbard. It looked like a relic from a distant age, but as Nathaniel turned he pulled out a gleaming blade.

"This, young squire, is *Scur-rida*, an old and trusted friend of mine, who I have happily not used for many a long year."

Hickory was confused, but Nathaniel met the boy's inquisitive gaze. "I have kept it hidden ever since we left Wyken Manor. You see, Hickory, a sword is a powerful thing and should only really be used when the need is there. I have kept it hidden under my cloak and at times it was very uncomfortable, not least when we made that ridiculous jump off Lincoln Cathedral, or when we rode upon the wild men through the North sea."

Hickory now took Nathaniel's sword and studied it. The blade was longer than his own but lighter and far, far older. Yet it was the handle that most intrigued him. The wooden pommel was almost black in colour and the wood twisted as if it had been carved by the wind.

"It's unusual isn't it?" Hickory nodded whilst he gave the weapon back to Nathaniel.

"The handle is made from the hull of the Venetian trading vessel which left me shipwrecked on the shores of the Holy Land, when I was first on crusade. I lost my own sword in the disaster so I had a new one forged in far-away Aleppo. I asked the master blacksmith to use a shaft of wood from the ship to remind me of my good fortune. I was the only survivor from the shipwreck you see."

Hickory's eyes widened in wonder, he knew little of England, let alone the Holy Land, but he had travelled over the sea and knew how frightening the wind and waves could be.

"But why is it called *Scur-rida*?" he asked.

Nathaniel smiled. "All swords should be named in the old tongue. In Anglo-Saxon, *scur* means storm and *rida* means rider so this is Storm-rider. It's an unusual name for a sword but I think it suits the story behind its making."

Hickory nodded in agreement. "So what about my sword?"

"Let's see if it can speak for itself shall we?" Nathaniel grinned.

"What do you mean?" Hickory was confused again.

The old man pulled the boy up from the floor. "Well, use it. Let's see it in action."

So Hickory twisted his sword in the rising moonlight and admired the way the blade cut through the night sky. "It looks like it could smash the heavens open, smite the moon and slay the sky."

"That's it then. Always go with your first instincts," Nathaniel told him.

Hickory turned the words around in his head and then said, "Sky-slayer, I like that!"

"So be it," replied Nathaniel with a smile. "Then, in the morning, as the first light of dawn touches the moor, into battle go *Scur-rida* and *Thur-brytta*. Storm-rider and Sky-slayer."

# Camlann Ridge
*~ Where Arthur fell, so legends tell~*

**M**orning broke quietly in the Green Knight's army encampment. No cockerel crowed, no birds sang. Instead, the only sounds that could be heard were those of war. Blades were sharpened, arrows placed in quivers, shield straps tightened and armour polished.

Hickory had awoken early and by the time Fern and Nathaniel had risen, he was already dressed in his mail shirt and the green surcoat of William d'Vert's army.

"So, you are going through with this?" Fern stood up from her bed, wrapped a blanket around her shoulders, and looked blankly at her brother.

"Yes, Fern," Hickory replied, "I must. I am part of this war, now."

"No, Hickory," she answered him, "you are part of nothing here. You belong far away from this. You belong under trees, in the heart of the woods. You belong with Father and me, not to some over-mighty Lord, who is full of pride and anger!"

"I am sorry, Fern, but I must see this through." Hickory grabbed his sword, picked up his shield and left the tent, ready for battle.

"I will watch over him, Fern. I will try to

keep him as far from the fighting as possible."
Nathaniel put on his own armour and strapped
Storm-rider to his belt.

"I know you will, Nathaniel. And I am
thankful for it." Fern wrapped her arms around
the old man.

"Now, I must go," he stared down at his
young friend.

"If you watch the battle, keep at a safe
distance."

"I will, Nathaniel," there were tears in
Fern's eyes now.

"And if all does not go well," he continued,
"then you must take Moon-shadow and ride east,
as fast as you can!"

With that the old man winked at her and
followed Hickory out into the sunlight and off to
war!

Outside their tent, the camp was in chaos!
Soldiers dashed this way and that, gathering
weapons, listening to orders and saying their
goodbyes.

Hickory made his way through this mass of
warriors and found Ethan d'Vert and Christian
de Troy, standing by their mounts.

"What are you doing?" Hickory watched

both of them gently place something in their horse's ears.

"It's candlewax," Ethan told him, "it stops the horse hearing the terrible sounds of battle and therefore they don't get too scared!"

Suddenly, a little figure bounded toward them. "He's coming," Penfric yelled to them as he ran out of the great pavilion, and sped over to the small gathering that stood outside the Green Knight's tent.

Moments later, William d'Vert strode out and handed a banner to Hickory. "Here it is then, lad. The battle standard of Cornwall. Hold it high, hold it steadfastly, like the rocks against the sea."

The old women who had sewn the new banner had only just finished it the night before. On one side of it was the flag of Cornwall, the black background and white cross of St Piran, the ancient saint of tin-miners. On the other side was the Green Knight's own device, the golden tree on the green background.

William d'Vert dressed in full armour and carrying a long sword at his side, stepped back away from Hickory and looked at the small assembly before him. His son was there, as was the captain of his bodyguard. Stood next to them was his squire and standard-bearer and then he gazed upon Nathaniel. "I see twelve notches on the pommel of your sword, old man. That is the kind of warrior I need today."

Hickory looked at his friend with new admiration, while Nathaniel stared down at the pommel and his gaze drifted away to ancient battles. "They are from the crusades, my Lord," he stated solemnly.

"You were a crusader?" d'Vert looked upon Nathaniel incredulously. With his ragged beard and crooked stance, the old man didn't look as though he could ever have been a knight.

"Yes. I was a Templar Knight. Blown by the winds to the Holy Land and back."

"What do you mean?" d'Vert asked.

Nathaniel smiled, "Many years ago I went on crusade. I foolishly believed that taking up arms could resolve a problem. Anyway, everywhere I travelled, it seemed as if the winds blew me on my way. Through southern France, I was pushed along by the warm *Mistral* and through Corsica by the wild *Libeccio*. In Italy, there was a wind they called *Tranontana* and it carried me down to the port of Bari. From there, my ship was blown by the *Levanter* all the way to the Holy Land."

"Well, I am proud to have a crusader in my ranks," d'Vert stated clearly. Then he mounted his horse and a trumpet call rallied his army to him.

The spring sunshine now lit the moor like a beacon and as Hickory looked far away to the south he could just see the shapes of horsemen many, many miles away. Nathaniel stared south too, but his eyes were not as good as the boy's.

"They are coming," Hickory said with a mixture of fear and excitement. "They are coming!"

Then, the trumpet sounded again and William d'Vert rode forward to address his army. To his right, in a straight line, stood the Company of Excalibur. Their armour was polished and their lances were raised up like a row of iron teeth. Behind them, were the men that would form the shieldwall. Tall and strong with large kite-shaped shields and armed with long swords and sharp axes. And to the left were the townsmen, fisherfolk and peasants. They would form the second ranks and do their best, with the little armour and meagre weapons that they had.

"Oaths were taken here long ago," d'Vert's voice rose up to the heavens. "Oaths that bound men to their King. And when that King fell, his men fell with him. Arthur they called him, and legends were written about him. Now, I ask you to bind yourselves to me. To make an oath that if I should fall, then you shall fall with me! Now, I ask you to become legends!"

The ranks of Cornish warriors beat their spears and swords against their shields and gave out a great cheer. Fern, peering out from behind the flap of her tent, watched with dismay as Hickory beat his own sword, and she noted with a heavy heart, the gleam of glory in his eyes.

Then the Green Knight's half-guard, the Company of Excalibur, led the Cornish army to the top of Camlann Ridge and they took up their positions and made ready for the battle to commence.

# 17. The Shieldwall

*~ Hard steel, chain-mail,*
*Hold fast and we won't fail*
*Eye to eye and shield to shield,*
*Let the weaker army yield*
*Stand proud, stand tall,*
*Stand behind the shieldwall ~*

**H**ickory stood in silence, watching the scene unfold below him in awe, as six thousand Breton warriors took their places in the battle line. Next to him stood Nathaniel. Nathaniel who had seen many battles and fought in countless skirmishes and Hickory was glad that the old man stood by him.

Down on the valley floor the Breton front line formed up. Here were squadrons of archers and crossbowmen. They wore no helmets upon their heads and few had mail shirts, but Hickory knew they were dressed for speed and agility. He also knew that when the order was given they would move swiftly forward and shoot their arrows high up the ridge toward them. Hickory thought back to Robin Hood's tales of the crusades and the damage wrought by the bowmen and he feared the coming onslaught of the iron rain.

Gathered in tightly packed lines behind the archers were the Breton infantry. Huge, fearsome figures they seemed to Hickory. Covered in long mail shirts and carrying axes and long swords, each man held a kite shield emblazoned with a black cross. Whilst they took up their positions they sang out a Breton war song that seemed to make the sky shudder.

At the back, slowly forming up, came the knights of Brittany; a thousand iron-clad warriors, their armour shimmering in the spring sunshine like the morning dew. As each Lord's standard was raised, a cheer went up from the horsemen and then in the centre, where the largest body of knights gathered, arose the black and silver banner of the Count of Brittany. Hickory couldn't make out the man himself amongst the warriors that swarmed around that flag, but he knew that somewhere down there was the man they called 'The Hammer'.

He turned to Nathaniel for reassurance and the old man smiled down at the boy, but then the trumpets sounded and Breton war cries split the air. Hickory looked back down upon the enemy ranks with dismay. He thought the Breton army looked terrifying, unbreakable...invincible. He gripped the Green Knight's banner tightly. He knew the time was coming, he knew he had to stand firm in the shieldwall, but his hands trembled as the fear took hold of him!

And then an odd thing happened, from behind Hickory a small figure pushed hurriedly past him and ran out from the shieldwall. He wore no armour and he carried no weapons, though his brightly coloured tunic sparkled in the morning light. It took a moment or two for Hickory to recognise the gawky little figure, but then he smiled, for it was Penfric, the Green Knight's aged jester.

Once he'd passed through the ranks he stood about thirty paces down the hill and shouted out some ancient Cornish insults at the Breton horde below. "Mos bod Bretonel keun!" he cried in Cornish and though Hickory didn't know it meant 'Go home Breton dogs,' it was clear that the Bretons did and they shouted back at Penfric in their common Celtic tongue.

Hickory didn't understand why the old fool wanted to rile the Bretons. They hardly needed stirring up! But as he watched him stride fearlessly down the hill toward the enemy, he had to admit that it was a brave, if foolhardy, act and somehow the madness of it lifted the spirits of the Cornish soldiers.

As Penfric danced in front of the Breton ranks he grinned at them and pulled faces and the men in the Cornish shieldwall laughed at the old jester. But as he turned back to face his own men, the Breton archers took aim. Their arrows flew swiftly and the smile fell from Penfric's face as the shafts thumped into his body. They tore through his red and green tunic and as blood trickled from his mouth, the old jester slumped to the ground.

Now it was the Bretons who cheered and shouted insults, whilst the Cornish shieldwall stood as one, united in their common cause. A cause brought suddenly and sharply into focus by the violent death of Penfric. Hickory stood tall with them and his fear left him to be replaced by another feeling. Revenge!

From the valley floor the Bretons barked out their orders and the front ranks of archers marched purposefully forward up the slope. The bowmen raised their weapons again, only this time they took aim at the Cornish shieldwall itself. Then it seemed to Hickory that the sky turned black with the iron rain and as he held up his shield to protect himself from the coming onslaught he knew that the battle had truly begun!

Arrow upon arrow fell upon the cowering men and to Hickory it felt as though some great beast was trying to bite through his shield. Shafts crashed into it with such velocity that he was

almost knocked over with the force. At one moment an arrowhead burst right through the wood, its iron tip just inches from the boy's face.

Hickory was not the only one recoiling in the wake of the arrow storm. All around him men were hiding behind their shields as the shafts fell down upon them and though the wall stood strong and the great shields offered protection, inevitably some of the arrows found their mark. Cries of pain rang out as men grasped helplessly at the bolts that tore through their mail-shirts and ripped into arms, legs and shoulders. Hickory wanted to drop his own shield and clasp his hands to his ears to stop the terrible noise of the suffering, but Nathaniel gripped his elbow and held him steady. And then as quickly as the arrow storm had started, it stopped again.

The soldiers who had fallen were pulled to the back of the shieldwall, whilst new warriors stepped forward to fill their places in the frontlines. Hickory and Nathaniel strode into the second rank and as they did so the Cornish warriors began to sing and chant in readiness for the next stage of the battle. For now a new menace had appeared!

# 18. Warwolf
## ~ *The King of Crows hides secret woes* ~

'Warwolf' the engineers had named it. For the menace that had appeared before them was a catapult. And it was enormous!

A solid construction of oak and iron, the trebuchet that was wheeled forward by twenty men, stood at the bottom of the ridge, and stared up defiantly at the thin Cornish line.

Horse-drawn carts were then brought up and stone missiles were left in an ominous pile. Six men then stepped forward and started to wind the ropes and load the deadly machine. The men on the hill looked down with a mixture of wonder and fear.

Then, 'Warwolf' began to fight. It hurled great chunks of stone with an angry twist of its gears and as it fired, the ground around the engine trembled. The boulders sailed through the air in a high arc and thundered into the Cornish ranks with a terrifying rage! Limbs were broken, bodies shattered and heads crushed as the stone missiles laid waste to the Cornish soldiers.

Something or somebody had to destroy the trebuchet before it won the battle on its own and from her vantage point on the edge of the trees to the west of Camlann Ridge, Fern knew this too.

She realised if she did not take part in the battle now, then her brother and Nathaniel would be soon buried under a hail of stone.

But what could she possibly do? What could anyone do against such a machine? Fern's gaze wandered away from the battlefield for a brief moment and then she heard a cry from the sky above and the instant she saw the bird hovering overhead she knew what to do.

"A chough," she mumbled. That is what Nathaniel named it, though the Cornish people called it 'The King of the Crows'. What was it that Penfric had told her? That the chough was the ancient King Arthur who fought here and that no-one dared shoot the bird for fear of killing the legendary King. Surely this was an omen! Perhaps he really had returned out of myth to save the day.

She called up to the bird in her own tongue and the chough twisted in the air and flew down to her. It landed at her feet and then strode up and down picking at the grubs under a loose piece of moss. All the while it fed it listened to Fern chatter away and then with a sudden squawk it took to the air once again.

On the battlefield no-one noticed the black bird as it flew toward the great trebuchet. The soldiers who were loading and re-loading the great engine were far too busy with their task and

even when the chough landed on 'Warwolf' itself they paid it no attention.

Up on the Cornish line the men could do nothing but pray that the next chunk of stone did not hit them. Hickory and Nathaniel stood there as firm as they could, though Hickory's belly quivered with fear as a huge lump of rock crashed into the shieldwall barely three feet away from him, sending four men tumbling to the ground in a tangle of mangled armour and broken bones.

Down upon 'Warwolf', the chough began to move. It hopped off the wheel arc and with a flutter of wings it landed softly on the great crossbeam at the top of the trebuchet. And then it started to peck. It pecked and pecked upon the ropes that held the firing lever to the rest of the siege weapon. Every few seconds it stopped and darted its head from side to side to check it had not been spotted and then it continued in its task.

From a distance it looked like some parasite on the shoulder of a huge beast and while the engineers carried on firing and the Breton army watched with glee as the Cornish shieldwall was battered, the chough continued to peck!

Another huge boulder was now brought forth. With a mighty heave the engineers loaded it in the trebuchet's firing sling and the trajectory of the firing lever was changed slightly. Up on the ridge, Hickory's far seeing eyes knew that the next shot would be aiming right at Nathaniel and himself.

The engineers pulled back the lever and pulled upon the winches, their muscles straining and their sinews pulling with might as they made ready to shoot. But just at the point of firing, the chough squawked and flew off the trebuchet. The engineers suddenly saw the bird and they looked upward at the crossbeam and spied the fraying ropes. Shouts of alarm suddenly rang out but it was too late, the chough had pecked through the ropes holding the crossbeam and as the men let go of the winch to fire, a great cracking noise splintered across the battlefield.

Wooden shafts and iron bolts were snapped and sent flying, knocking the engineers to the floor in a hail of debris. Then, with an almighty crash 'Warwolf', the great trebuchet, thundered to the ground in a mangled heap of shattered wood and steel. A cheer rose from the Cornish line and Hickory smiled in relief as he watched the beast fall below him.

At the trees edge, Fern whispered her thanks to the chough as the King of the Crows caught the morning breeze and rose high above the battlefield and disappeared back into the clouds.

The Cornish line, however, had little time to celebrate and as they plugged the gaps that the catapult had made in the shiedwall, they prepared once again for another onslaught. For marching up Camlann Ridge towards them was the Breton infantry!

# 19. The Last Charge
## ~ Ride at the enemy, ride, ride! ~

At the sight of the marching Bretons, the Cornish soldiers began to bellow out insults and cries of defiance, "Out, out, out!" they cried and they beat the backs of their shields with the pommels of their swords. Then, as the Breton warriors closed the ground between them and began to charge, the shieldwall braced itself for impact.

The collision was ferocious! Shields splintered, axes were swung, swords were stabbed and spears were thrown. Even in the second rank back, Hickory and Nathaniel felt the force of the attack and they recoiled back a pace with the rest of the line. Yet the front rank of the Cornish shieldwall held firm and though the Bretons fought with vigour, they could not find a way through the wall of shields.

To howls of delight from the Cornish soldiers, the Bretons pulled away and dragging their fallen comrades they drew back down the hill. From behind Hickory an order was given and arrows flew from the handful of Cornish archers that the Green Knight had kept in reserve. His timing had been perfect, for with their backs turned the arrows knocked many of the retreating

Bretons to the ground.

◦❦◦❦◦❦◦

The sun now began to climb high overhead and the white clouds above began to dance across the sky as a breeze swept over Camlann Ridge. Below the shieldwall, the Breton army re-grouped; the Count's first two assaults upon the Cornish line had come to nothing, but the men on the ridge knew that Robert Guiscard was not a man who gave up easily. Hickory and Nathaniel watched and waited with the rest of the warriors, all the time wondering what 'The Hammer' would try next.

It didn't take long! A barking of orders saw the Breton archers and infantry march to the back of the enemy lines and down on the valley floor the horsemen rode forward. Hooves splashed in the stream, the Breton knights raised their lances and the cavalry began to make their way ominously up the lower slopes of the hill.

It was an awesome sight; a thousand mail-clad knights, their banners rippling in the morning breeze like the sails of a sea-bound armada. Hickory had never seen anything like it! The coats-of-arms of a multitude of different families fluttered before him; golden lions, silver fleur-de-lys, white griffins and black ravens, all leaping in the sky. And somewhere he was sure he saw a white dragon!

The Breton knights now formed up into a great wedge formation; an arrowhead to smash through the shieldwall on the ridge. And at the heart of it was Robert Guiscard himself, his half-guard of knights around him, the black and silver striped banners of Brittany flying high. Then, as one, they lowered their lances and galloped up the hill.

On the top of Camlann Ridge, William d'Vert knew he had to react quickly to this new threat and he spoke hurriedly with his advisors.

"There is only one choice left, my Lord," Christian de Troy stated.

"I know," d'Vert replied with a heavy heart. He knew the men that he would send forward now, had no hope. And he knew he was sending his own son and his closest friends to their end.

"Shall I lead them?" de Troy looked searchingly into the Green Knight's eyes.

D'Vert paused for a moment, as he watched a seagull arc above them. Then, he cast his eyes back to the approaching enemy horsemen. "Yes, de Troy, you should lead them," he replied thoughtfully. "And tell them they carry the hopes of Cornwall with them".

Christian de Troy bowed his head in reply, pulled on the reins of his horse and left the Green

Knight's side.

A few moments later trumpets sounded behind the Cornish lines. Then, the shieldwall opened and a small band of a hundred or so horsemen rode out to a chorus of cheers. For even though they were few in number, they inspired hope in the soldiers on the hilltop.

They had their own banners and pennants to rival those of the approaching Bretons too. Most prominent was the flag of St Patrin, but there were red dragons, golden falcons and rampant lions also. Some coats-of-arms even mirrored those in the Breton army, for family ties had been broken by this war.

Hickory could see the green pennant of the d'Vert household and the blue of Lyonesse too and he watched Ethan d'Vert and Christian de Troy with pride as they rode out and then he smiled as they levelled their lances and prepared to charge.

Hickory saw de Troy take something from his saddle. It glimmered briefly in the morning sunlight and then he held it to his mouth.

"It's a shell," Nathaniel whispered to him, "a last reminder from Lyonesse."

De Troy blew the shell like a trumpet and as the sound filled the air he rose from his saddle and addressed the small band of knights. "Dyw genes Kernow!" he shouted and then they all shouted with him.

"Dyw genes Kernow! God be with you Cornwall!" they cried.

Then, Christian de Troy led them down the hill. Straight at the heart of the oncoming Breton knights. Straight for 'The Hammer' himself!

# 20. Slaughterbridge

*~ When the battlefield turns red, the ravens will be fed~*

The impact was tremendous and though Hickory wanted to look away as his friends ploughed down the slope and into the Breton ranks, he found he could not take his eyes off the shattering sight. Lances were thrust, maces swung and enemy horsemen were sent sprawling, as Christian de Troy and his noble band of knights pierced the Breton cavalry like a silver arrow.

But their initial success was soon halted. Outnumbered ten to one by the enemy horsemen, the Cornish knights soon found themselves surrounded. Their valiant charge had come to nothing and Hickory watched with growing sadness as one by one the brave hundred were cut down. He shuddered as he saw Ethan d'Vert's body hit the bloody ground and then he gasped aloud as the blue banner of Lyonesse fell. Christian de Troy and the Company of Excalibur lay dying!

With a whoop of exhilaration, the Breton knights now took up a charge of their own. Hastily re-forming, they drove their horses up Camlann Ridge and straight for the wavering shieldwall.

"Stand firm lad," Nathaniel's voice was barely audible as the Cornish soldiers once again beat their shields. "Stand firm and hold your shield steady. If we all interlink our shields, then nothing will break us."

Hickory looked along the line and saw that the men in their rank of the shieldwall had done just that, so he moved one pace to the right and overlapped the soldier's shield that was next to him. Nathaniel in turn overlapped his and they stood as one.

It was the rank in front of him that took the brunt of the Breton cavalry's attack and when it came it smashed upon them like a whirlwind. And yet somehow the line still held. A bulwark of wood and steel manned with the determination of grim men. The Breton knights continued to wheel up and down the Cornish shieldwall, but they could find no way through.

The shieldwall breathed a sigh of relief as the Breton army re-grouped once again. This time both the Breton cavalry and foot soldiers charged up the hill. Robert Guiscard himself led this final assault and the men in the shieldwall braced themselves once more.

Nathaniel and Hickory had filled the gap in the front line now and half a mile away Fern's gaze picked them out, as she stood helpless. She reached out to touch the leaves of the silver birch tree that stood beside her, for comfort, and then she shut her eyes.

The impact, however, was not as hard as Hickory and the old man had expected. In fact the Cornish line not only held firm but they began to beat the Bretons back down the slope with ease.

"Victory is here for the taking!" cried William d'Vert, who stood in the centre of the depleted shieldwall. As the Breton soldiers in front of him turned to flee, the Green Knight and his bodyguard broke ranks from the shieldwall and followed them down the slope.

All around Hickory, Cornish warriors followed suit and started to unlock their shields and chase the fleeing Bretons back down the ridge. Without thinking Hickory now did the same.

"No," screamed Nathaniel, "it's a trap!" But it was too late. Driven forward by the thrill of the battle and the scent of victory, Hickory followed the warriors who pursued the Bretons down the hill. He dropped his shield altogether, held the Green Knight's banner high and drew Sky-slayer! "Victory," he roared with the others and he ran down the hill.

Yet Nathaniel was right. He knew how King Harold had lost his crown at the Battle of Hastings and here he saw it repeated again, for halfway down the slope the retreating Bretons turned in a pre-planned counter-attack and cut down the pursuing Cornish soldiers. Small bands of Cornishmen now lay trapped in the open, their shieldwall rendered useless. The promise of triumph now lay in ruins and defeat now stared the Cornish army in the face.

Hickory looked across Camlann Ridge and everywhere he gazed he saw clusters of Cornish soldiers standing like silver islands in a sea of Breton warriors. Hundreds of men now lay trapped out on the hillside. Even the Green Knight and his bodyguard were drowning under the surge of the counter-attack. He closed his eyes for a brief moment and wished he was back in the greenwood. But when he opened them again he was in the midst of slaughter and charging straight at him, intent on capturing the Green Knight's standard, was a huge Breton knight!

Hickory recoiled at the sight of the charging warrior and then as the knight turned his black shield toward him, Hickory gasped as he saw the device upon it. It was a white dragon, which meant that the warrior rushing toward him was none other than Ranulf de Roche!

Holding his sword high above his head, de Roche came upon Hickory and swung his blade downwards. It crashed upon the boy's upturned shield with a mighty thud! The impact knocked Hickory to the ground and the Green Knight's banner went tumbling.

From the corner of his eye, Nathaniel had seen Hickory fall. Realising de Roche was about to finish the boy, he rushed down the hill, twisted his arm and shoved his own shield into de Roche's shoulder. The blow knocked de Roche away from Hickory, but then he turned upon the old man, bellowed an insult and whipped his sword across Nathaniel's face.

The sword hit Nathaniel hard, splintering against his helmet, sending tiny shards of steel up into his eyes. The old man dropped his shield and threw his hands to his face. Then, he fell down next to Hickory with a howl of pain.

De Roche now stood over both of them. He picked up the Green Knight's standard from the bloody ground and smiled. Then he thrust his blade down at the lying body of Hickory. But somehow, Hickory managed to roll away from the attack. Then, as de Roche raised his weapon for another blow, Hickory gripped *Sky-slayer*, closed his eyes and lunged the sword upwards.

Ranulf de Roche was not expecting the assault and Hickory's blade ripped upward through de Roche's mailshirt and tore into his belly.

Stumbling backwards in agony, de Roche suddenly found himself in the path of a band of mounted knights. The horses reared up before him and then he was knocked to the ground. The knights rode over the fallen de Roche and he screamed out as the horses trampled him underfoot. Lying just a few feet away from him, Hickory now watched, as de Roche's fingers loosened around the Green Knight's standard, and then de Roche's last breath left his body.

Hickory pulled himself up onto his knees and crawled over to Nathaniel. All around him the slaughter continued unabated, but he ignored it and pushed back the old man's helmet to see what damage had been done. Hurriedly, he wiped away the blood that covered his friend's face, only to recoil at what he saw. Steel shards from de Roche's sword had embedded themselves in the old man's eyes and Hickory felt devastated as he realised that Nathaniel had been blinded!

He threw up his hands in horror. This had

been his fault! It was his passion for war that had led them to this. He should have listened to Fern. They should have left Cornwall days ago, and then this would not have happened. He buried his face in the old man's chest and under his helmet, tears streamed down his face.

And then, something strange happened. The grass around Hickory and Nathaniel grew. Green tips sprouted, long stalks rose up and within minutes, the old man and the boy were safely hidden from the bloodshed around them. It was as if Hickory's outpouring of grief and his need for redemption had forced nature to accept him back into its domain.

It was all too much for the green boy. His mind swam, his eyes closed and as more shapes now moved across the battlefield, shadows of warriors seemed to rise up out of a dream.

Hickory was now struggling to stay conscious, the pain in his head was plunging him into darkness. He felt himself falling, falling.

Suddenly, a young knight appeared in front of him. He bent low and lifted the visor of Hickory's helmet. His eyes smiled down at the fallen boy and then amidst the chaos of the battlefield, he spoke calmly and gently, "take my hand, Pignut!" he said.

The words shook Hickory from his pain. Was this all a dream? But then, he suddenly realised who his saviour was.

"It can't be you!" Hickory gasped. "It can't be!"

# 21. Old Friends

*~ Help often comes when least expected~*

From the edge of the trees, Fern had watched in horror, when Hickory and Nathaniel fell under the weight of the Breton onslaught. She had forced herself to turn away from the battlefield, to look east and think about how she would escape this disaster. But then, on the far horizon she saw a new cluster of banners appear and hope rose within her again.

At first, she had thought it was another Breton assault, a new attack that would bring the battle of Camlann Ridge to a decisive end. Yet, something had stirred within her, something inside had told her that the hundreds of men that marched toward the battle were not the enemy. And then she saw the banner that led the attack, and immediately she recognised the device upon it. A white ship on a blue background. The coat of arms of her old friend Richard de Calne, the man who had taken care of them back in Suffolk.

She stared at this new army in disbelief. And then, with her keen eyes, she saw Sir Richard himself, riding at the head of a band of knights and leading his men straight at the Breton lines.

Behind Sir Richard, her heart leapt again to

see Cob Fletcher. He was shouting orders to a line of archers and she watched with pride as Tam One-eye, Bull Weaver and other familiar faces from the village of Woolpit, loosed their arrows upon the enemy. She tried to shout to Cob but she was too far away and her slender voice was lost amongst the cries of battle.

Outflanked and caught by surprise, the Breton army were stunned by this sudden turn of events. The men from Suffolk had smashed into their rear and the Bretons now found themselves surrounded.

Robert Guiscard and his bodyguard were fighting furiously, trying to capture the Green Knight and finish off the remnants of the Company of Excalibur, when they were caught completely off-guard.

On the brink of victory, the Breton army now fell apart. Men began to run. They threw down their shields, dropped their swords and fled. Guiscard held together his knights and they stood firm in the middle of the field, but he swore as his army fell around him.

"Truce?" William d'Vert caught sight of his half-brother in the midst of battle and shouted to him. "Truce, Robert!" he cried.

'The Hammer' pulled up his visor and stared coldly back at d'Vert. He surveyed the scene before him. With the arrival of this new army no one could win this battle now, he knew that. Then he saw Richard de Calne cutting a path toward him. His knights were fresh and it was de Calne that had the upper hand now. Guiscard did not know who this new enemy was, but he knew that defeat stared him in the face. "Truce," he shouted back to d'Vert and then suddenly all the soldiers around them heard the word and they stopped fighting.

"Truce," they all now cried, "truce!" And across the bloody field of battle, warriors lay down their weapons and fell upon the ground exhausted.

The battle of Camlann Ridge was over!

# 22. Healing Hands
*~ Not all wounds can be cured~*

When nightfall came to Bodmin Moor, all the tents of the Green Knight's camp were crammed with wounded soldiers. And in many of them, both Cornishmen and Breton lay side by side.

The surgeons and the healers had been kept active, but none were busier than Fern. She had tended each wound and had run herself ragged for many hours. Now, as the last of the injured men were brought to the camp, she caught her breath and made her way to the small tent by the western gate, in which lay her brother and Nathaniel.

But when she lifted the flap and let her eyes become accustomed to the candlelight, the face she encountered, standing vigil over her brother, surprised her. She crossed quickly to Hickory's bed, fearful of the shape that stood over him.

"Simeon de Calne," Hickory mumbled, looking up at the face before him, "Simeon de Calne!"

"Yes, Hickory," the reply came, "it is me, but perhaps not the Simeon you remember." The young knight smiled as Fern approached them.

"Look Fern," Hickory turned his eyes up to

meet his sister's gaze.

"I can see who it is, Hickory," she stated warily.

"He saved me," the boy spoke in wonder. "He did!"

"Was I so awful before?" Simeon grinned.

"Yes," Fern replied coldly, "you were!"

"Then, I am sorry for the way I behaved back at Wyken," Simeon answered her. "That was almost a year ago and much has changed since then."

Fern looked upon Simeon with a studied gaze. He looked different somehow. He was a young man now. He had grown into his body and he stood before them like a young tree. Tall and straight and unwavering.

"Yes," she spoke softly, "I do believe much has changed since then." Fern looked down at her brother and across to the sleeping form of Nathaniel in the next bed.

"It's my doing, isn't it?" Hickory followed his sister's gaze toward the old man.

Fern bit her lip, she knew that Hickory's desire had led them here, but what boy wouldn't have been bewitched by the Green Knight? She could not blame him and she knew Nathaniel would not either.

"No, Hickory. It is not your doing. Now, close your eyes and get some sleep." She kissed him gently on his forehead and he shut his eyes.

Simeon then took her arm and guided her away from Hickory's bed. "Fern," he spoke firmly, "you must speak with my father, urgently."

"Why?" Fern looked worried.

"He will tell you. Now, go quickly to the Green Knight's pavilion."

Though Fern had been busy all evening, healing many of the fallen, the battlefield was still littered with many that were beyond even her skills.

One of these was Christian de Troy. He had been found lying next to his horse, for the great steed that had carried him to safety all those years ago, was also dead. And so it was that the last link to the ancient Kingdom of Lyonesse was broken forever. Christian de Troy had no son to carry on his name and so that day, Lyonesse finally succumbed to its fate.

Yet the line of the House of d'Vert would continue. For young Ethan d'Vert, to the delight of his father, had not been slain. His arm was broken and there was a nasty looking gash on his right thigh, but Fern had put a poultice of honey and willow-herb on his arm and strapped a bandage around his leg and with time and care he would mend well enough.

"Thank God, you're safe lad. Your mother would never have forgiven me!" William d'Vert was sat beside the outstretched form of his son. He stroked his temple, as Ethan slipped in and out of a fitful sleep.

Then, d'Vert rose from his son's bed and crossed the floor of the great pavilion to meet the tall knight that now entered the tent.

"I do not know how to thank you," William d'Vert smiled as he shook the hand of Sir Richard de Calne. "Cornwall is forever in your debt."

"I did not come for Cornwall," Sir Richard replied. "I came for the children and the old man, though I am glad to have helped defend a part of England from foreign invasion."

"Well, for whatever reason you came here, I am glad of it," d'Vert stated.

When Fern made her way toward the great pavilion, someone called her name through the darkness. By the light of a glowing fire, a man sat, chewing a piece of waybread and sipping a mug of beer.

Beside him two other men slept noisily. "They've had too much ale," the man smiled through the gloom.

"Oh Cob," Fern exclaimed as she suddenly realised who the man was, "I have missed you," she said as she felt herself wrapped up in his great arms.

"Martha and I have missed you too, girl." He put her down and wiped a stray strand of hair from her face.

"Not to mention, Till and Meg. I had to throw Till out of the back of one of the wagons, to stop him from coming. He's become a good archer, but he is too young yet, to fight in a battle."

"How did you know we were here?" Fern sat by him as Tam One-eye and Bull Weaver snored away.

"Master Drinkstone, of course," Cob answered. "Old Nathaniel sent a letter to Sir Richard explaining your plight. 'Trapped in Cornwall and about to be defeated by the Breton army,' so his message said. Within two days Sir Richard had raised enough troops and we began our march here."

Fern smiled, it was just like Nathaniel to save the day. What would they have done without the old man? How could they have come this far?

"Poor Nathaniel," Fern's gaze glanced back to the old man's tent. "I do not think he will ever see again. I have tried all I know but the wound is too deep. There is no infection, but his eyes are damaged beyond my skill."

"I know girl, and it will hit him hard. A man of letters like that." Cob followed her gaze.

"Hickory blames himself," Fern sighed, and her eyes looked into the flames.

"No use in that," Cob said. "We are all responsible for our own actions. Nathaniel is not a man to hold a grudge."

"No," Fern tore her gaze away from the flickering flames, "and Hickory will make amends. I am sure of that."

Cob stood up now, and helped the girl to her feet.

"Nathaniel's letter was not the only thing that brought us here, Fern."

"What do you mean?" Fern's face took on an anxious look.

"Sir Richard will explain all to you." Cob stroked her face again. "Now get yourself away to him."

Fern turned away from Cob and looked toward the great pavilion. Candles shimmered within and the sound of many voices could be heard inside the tent.

She found herself almost running toward it now and when she entered, she saw what looked like a makeshift hospital. There were many beds inside, for the Green Knight's men had been housed within and healers scurried this way and that, attending to the wounded soldiers.

She searched hurriedly for the face of Sir Richard de Calne, but she could not spot him. And then, from somewhere behind her, she heard his voice.

"Fern!" he cried as he broke away from his conversation with William d'Vert and came to meet her. "It's so good to see you again."

"Sir Richard," Fern replied as she bowed before him.

"Do not be so formal," he smiled, and lifted her into his arms.

"Thank you for coming to rescue us, Sir Richard. I feared the worst as I watched the battle from the trees."

He ushered her to a chair to rest by the fireside. "I could not let you get into too much mischief could I?" Sir Richard sat next to her and turned his chair to face her. "Besides, I have important news for you."

"Cob told me you wanted to speak to me urgently," Fern's eyes searched Sir Richard's face for information.

"Yes," Sir Richard spoke softly now and placed his hands upon her shoulders, "it's your father, Fern. He's been found!"

She almost jolted out of the chair with

shock. Since discovering that the Green Knight was not their father, she'd thought all was lost. But here was hope rekindled, once again. And this time it was not just some story about a mythical character, but actual fact. Her father had been found!

"But something's wrong?" Fern watched as the colour drained from Sir Richard's face.

"You do not miss a thing do you?" de Calne answered her enquiring gaze. "But you are right, something is very wrong. You see, your father has been captured by the Abbot."

The stern features of Guy de Bellambe, the Abbot of Bury St Edmunds, suddenly flickered through her mind. Her one encounter with the clergyman was not something she had easily forgotten.

"We must leave tomorrow," Sir Richard continued, "and make all haste for Suffolk."

"What will the Abbot do to him?" Fern's face looked anxious.

"I do not know, Fern," Sir Richard paused, "but you know what kind of a man the Abbot is. I fear the worst."

"Then, I must get ready," she cried.

"You must rest first," William d'Vert stated. "You have worked yourself to near exhaustion, helping the men."

"And what will happen with the Bretons

now?" Fern looked up at the Green Knight who stood nearby and her eyes seemed to pierce his heart. The loss of so many men had shaken his pride and it was a different man that stared back at her. Gone was the air of invincibility, gone was the arrogance. Instead, here stood a man ready to negotiate, a man ready to end the war.

"In the morning, I will meet with my half-brother," the Green Knight stated firmly, "and we will make peace!"

"Good," Fern replied, "I am pleased."

Back in his own tent, lying in his bed and listening to the snores of the old man next to him, Hickory realised that the war had changed him too. No longer did he dream of charging into battle. Now he knew that the battlefield was not a place of glory, but one of fear and terror. Not a dream, but a nightmare and one that should be avoided at all costs. A man's life was worth more than that!

And with that thought, he slipped to sleep and dreamt once again of the greenwood, and the trees and the wild creatures that lived there.

# 23. The Truce of Bodmin
~ *Give and take, forget and forgive*
*In peace we trust, in peace we live* ~

"He is outside my Lord," the guard addressed William d'Vert, who was adjusting his surcoat. He wanted to look his best for this occasion.

"Thank you, I will be out shortly." The guard left the tent with a bow and d'Vert readied himself.

"It is the right thing to do, Father," Ethan d'Vert handed his father his sword and the Green Knight looked deep into his son's eyes.

"I know, Ethan," the Green Knight replied. "The absence of Penfric's laughter and Christian's wise counsel, remind me only too well of the need for peace. They would still be here was it not for my pride."

"They fought for you, Father, because they believed in you. You and Cornwall. But it is right now to sue for peace," Ethan answered.

"Come then, let us meet our enemy," d'Vert smiled at his son, "and make him our friend, again."

Outside, a table had been set up and upon it was a manuscript entitled 'The Truce of Bodmin.' Next to it was an ink well and a quill pen.

Scribes and priests stood close by to ratify the agreement, once the men had agreed upon it.

Robert Guiscard was there too, surrounded by a circle of Breton knights who stood aside as d'Vert approached.

"Well, I am here, William. As you requested." Guiscard spoke with calm authority, although he knew he had almost been defeated the day before.

"I am glad you came. We have fought each other to a standstill. It is time to end this now," d'Vert strode to the table and picked up the quill pen. "You have read the peace treaty, Robert?"

"Yes," Guiscard replied, "it is satisfactory."

"Good. Then shall we?" d'Vert signed his name to the bottom of the document and handed the pen to his half-brother. Guiscard dipped the quill in the ink and added his own name.

Hands were shaken, then each man waited while a scribe dripped red wax onto the bottom of the treaty. Then, Robert Guiscard, and following him William d'Vert, each took their seals and placed them in the wax. And so it was that 'The Hammer' and the 'Golden Tree' became entwined in the red wax. Joined as one. Cornwall and Brittany, together once more.

The soldiers watching the event cheered and broke out into song. First the Bretons sang, then the Cornishmen joined them, for the songs they sang and the words they spoke were so alike.

That night, before they headed back to Suffolk
the next morning, there was one thing left for
Hickory to do. He went alone on Starlight and
they darted across the open moor-land like a
speeding arrow.

At the southern edge of the moor they came
to a halt, high up on a windswept plain. Hickory
dismounted from the horse and then took
something from his saddlebag. He moved slowly
across the grass like a ghost and then he made his
way down to the dark waters of a lake.

A faint crescent moon shone through the
thin clouds above and then a bird flew close to the
boy's head. It made Hickory jump; it was
unusual to see birds during the night. But,
Hickory swore it was the same one he had seen at
the battle the previous day. The chough, Fern had
called it, but whatever it was and whoever it may
once have been, it disappeared into the black
night.

Down by the edge of the lake, the dark
waters lapped softly against the reeds and a
ghostly mist hung over the pool like a shroud.
Hickory unwrapped the object he had taken from
his saddlebag. The blade of *Sky-slayer* glinted in

the moonlight.

He took one final look at the sword, turned and twisted it in the air and breathed its name over it as if it were magic. Then, he held *Sky-slayer* behind his head, arched his body backward and threw the sword as far as he could into the murky waters of Dozmary Pool.

The sword flew far out into the middle of the lake and splashed into the water. Hickory thought he saw something. Was it a floating branch or was it something else? A hand perhaps, reaching up and taking the sword to the depths below. Hickory couldn't tell what it was, but as the blade disappeared beneath the water, he swore never to take up arms again.

He whistled to Starlight, mounted the horse with a leap and rode back across the moors to Fern, Nathaniel and his friends.

The children and Nathaniel, together with Sir Richard and the others, left at daybreak, the following morning. The remnants of the Cornish army turned out to see them on their way and there were cries of thanks and cheers of goodbye as the soldiers and the wagons of the troops from Suffolk marched away.

About half-way across Bodmin Moor they

passed a cottage. Inside they could hear a woman singing whilst she baked bread. Then, from behind a line of washing, a boy ran out and gave Fern a ragged bunch of moorland flowers. He grinned at the procession that was passing his home, grabbed an apple from one of the wagons and skipped away again. Fern and Hickory laughed as they waved back at the grinning face of Gebbedy!

And so the green children and the men of Sir Richard de Calne's army began the long march home to the green fields and wide skies of Suffolk.

Further west, off the far tip of the Cornish coast, where the waves lap against the sands, a red sun slowly rose into the western sky. Here Ethan d'Vert and a handful of men took a wooden box from the back of a wagon.

They carried it carefully to the edge of the cliffs, near to where the land ends. Ethan d'Vert said a few solemn words in the ancient Cornish language and then, taking a corner each, the men threw the coffin off the edge.

The wooden box fell a hundred feet into the crashing waves below. It bobbed up and down for a brief moment as if it were trying to swim. But then it slipped under the waves. The men on top of the cliff bowed their heads as Christian de Troy returned home to Lyonesse.

A mile or so further down the coast the Breton fleet pulled up anchor and turned their sails to home also.

The war in Cornwall had ended!

# Part Two

## The Holly Crown

When summer comes the world turns green,

out come the faerie King and Queen.

They sit in majesty and might,

In the shadow of the night.


Then, the power of the trees,

will bring their foes to their knees.

For the one who wears the Holly crown

Has the power to strike his enemies down.

# 24. Angel Hill

*~ At the end of the rope, there is still hope~*

soft summer rain fell upon the heads of the crowd as they made their way noisily down Angel Hill. At the bottom of the slope, they congregated in the large cobbled square, outside the gates of the great Abbey of Bury St Edmunds.

There were hundreds of people gathered here, for there hadn't been this much excitement in the town since the bread riots of three years ago. What a day that had been!

And now, here was excitement again. A trial. And not just of some common horse thief or sly pickpocket. Oh no, this was the trial of a King!

It had taken the best part of four days to get back to Suffolk and even then Fern, Hickory, Sir Richard, Simeon and Cob Fletcher had needed to leave the main body of the army behind and ride on ahead.

They were exhausted by the time they saw Wyken Manor. But speed was of the essence. Who knew what Guy de Bellambe had planned for the children's father? Though Sir Richard was sure, it would be something unpleasant!

After resting briefly and taking fresh horses from the stables, they soon found themselves approaching Bury St Edmunds itself. On a rise, just outside the town, they stared down at the spire of the great abbey. It rose high above the thatched roofs, pointing skyward, like a great stone finger. Pointing to God himself so many said. But it was from far below the spire that the people of Bury now came.

Even from their position, almost half a mile away, Fern and Hickory could see the townspeople striding toward the square. "Quick!" Fern cried to the others, "something's happening down there." She pointed, but the others' sight was not as good as hers or her brother's, and they saw only the outlines of the buildings and the abbey's towers.

Yet, they knew she was right, they all felt the tension around them, the lull that comes before a great storm. So they pulled hard on their reins and rode down toward the abbey.

By the time they had tethered their horses in the Buttermarket and joined the crowd, it was clear that something important was going on, for they found themselves being pushed all the way down

Churchgate Street and into the open square of Angel Hill.

Here, in the middle of the square, directly in front of the abbey gates, they saw that a wooden scaffold had been erected. Standing in the centre of the stage was the Abbot, Guy de Bellambe, his long black robes flowing down like a raven's wings. His stern face showed no sign of emotion and his cold eyes stared out at the quietening crowd.

Monks and guards scurried around on the scaffold behind the Abbot, but next to him were two other men. They had rich silk tunics on, but their faces were hidden under their hoods. They whispered to each other whilst the Abbot clicked his fingers and called the guards to bring out his prisoner.

The crowd now fought for standing room, pushing and shoving in their eagerness to catch sight of the figure that was brought forth. He was tall, they could all see that, though his head was bowed. His hands had been tied behind his back and he shuffled along very slowly, for his ankles had also been chained together. Yet, despite his shackles and his simple tunic of green cloth, there was something noble and proud about the strange prisoner.

Then, the mob gasped as one, as they saw the green face that stared back out at them. Some started to scream and shout abuse at him, others pelted him with rotten fruit.

But in the far corner of the square, one group of onlookers reacted very differently, for when Fern and Hickory looked upon the green face of the prisoner, they shuddered.

"Father," Fern cried, "my Father!" She turned her face from the scene and almost fell against Sir Richard. Hickory too, was stricken with worry and he gripped Cob's hand so hard, that the villager winced.

The face that stared out at the mob below was a noble face. As green as the children's, but etched with lines across his forehead. A greying beard framed his face and clear, steely-grey eyes stared out at the crowd. At his throat was a necklace of berries and upon his head was a crown of holly leaves. A crown that marked him out as a king.

The children searched their father's face and slowly the faint images of memory came back to them. They wanted to call out to him, tell him they were there in the crowd. They wanted to help him, take him away from this baying mob, run with him back into the safety of the trees. But they knew this was not the moment to act.

Then, the two hooded figures behind the Abbot came to the front of the scaffold, to stand by de Bellambe.

"Who is that next to the Bishop?" Fern asked anxiously as she gathered her emotions.

"I don't know," whispered Simeon.

The slimmer of the hooded figures moved slowly away from the Bishop and toward the Green King. As he approached him he seemed to speak to him, but from their place in the crowd, they could not hear what he said.

"Oh no!" cried Fern as her fingers tightened upon Hickory's shoulder. His eyes followed hers, as the bony figure suddenly pulled down his hood. "It's him!" Fern exclaimed in shock. "It's Silas of Wickham!"

Hickory couldn't believe his eyes but his sister was right! For the scarred face of the witchfinder who had pursued them to Orford last year, stared silently up at the waiting noose.

And then the other figure next to the witchfinder pulled down his hood. It was Sir Richard and his son who now looked shocked. "Thomas Galliard!" Simeon exclaimed. "What's he doing here?"

"So they've joined forces, have they?" Sir Richard stared at his old steward with disdain. After getting him to release his claws from his son, he'd often wondered what had become of him. Now, it was clear, he had somehow hooked up with Silas of Wickham.

The witchfinder strode to the edge of the

scaffold and looked down at the crowd with a sneer. Then, he pointed at the Green King, "Look at his crown," he cried out, with a snarl, "a false imitation of the crown of thorns worn by Jesus."

The crowd babbled in response.

"Who does he think he is?" Wickham continued, eyeing the circlet of leaves on the Green King's head. "Do we not put holly around our houses to keep the witches away? And here, he flaunts his wickedness, by wearing a crown made of the stuff!"

"So what shall we do with the heathen?" the Abbot shouted, trying to whip up the crowd even further.

"Hang him!" bellowed someone from the mob below.

"String up the green devil!" screamed another.

"We will not hang him straight away," Silas of Wickham answered the shout, "he must be properly tried. A trial by ordeal would seem fair to me. What say you, Abbot?"

"Yes indeed, Lord Witchfinder. God will tell us what to do with this evil creature." The Abbot's voice struck terror into the children's hearts.

"Bring forth the poker," Wickham commanded.

Underneath the scaffold, a fire was lit and

then an abbey guard took an iron poker and laid it in the red flames. He waited silently for a few moments, whilst the whole crowd seemed to hold its breath.

When it was deemed hot enough, Wickham ordered the guard to remove the poker from the fire and bring it up to him.

The Green King's face showed no reaction as Wickham moved towards him. "Hold out his hand!" Wickham shouted and the two guards that held the King forced him to open his hand, palm upward.

With a grin Silas said, "Let us see if he is a witch," and he pushed the poker down onto the King's hand.

Fern fought back a scream and Hickory closed his eyes, but the King himself remained unmoved. He stared out defiantly and Wickham grew angry when his victim did not even flinch with the pain.

The crowd cheered at first, but as they saw how nobly the Green King dealt with the torture they quietened down. Then, Wickham pulled the poker up again and held the King's hand up to the crowd. "His green skin is red and blistered!" he shouted, but the crowd did not respond. "He is a witch. He tries to deceive us. He allows us to harm him. But I know his ways. He holds a black allegiance to the devil."

Fern, stared in horror. She could take no more. Quickly, she slipped away from the others and ran to the far side of the square, where she found a tall statue of the martyred King Edmund. Hurriedly, she climbed the stone King and looked down upon the crowd and the trial.

"He holds no allegiance to the devil," she cried out in desperation. Her voice was brave, strong and resolute and yet as tender as the lark. She would not lose her father again, not now she had found him at last.

The crowd turned to stare up at her. Many of them gasped to see another green face amongst them. Some grew afraid but others heard her plea, "He does not even know who your Jesus is! His crown is his own. It is no imitation. He is a good and decent man."

On hearing her voice, the Green King himself looked up to see his daughter defending him. Their eyes met for a brief moment, a moment of calm in a sea of turbulence. Then, a guard cuffed the King across the face and he turned his gaze reluctantly back down to the floor of the scaffold.

But amongst the crowd that listened to Fern's appeal were people from the village of Woolpit and the surrounding farms that owed their allegiance to Sir Richard. They recognised Fern and cheered her words and many of them now began to shout in the Green King's defence.

"Let him go!" one shouted.

"He has done nothing wrong!" hollered another.

The villagers from Sir Richard's lands began to push their way to the front of the crowd. Jostling broke out between them and the townsfolk, who still wanted the Green King executed. The Abbot saw the commotion and called the abbey guards to the front of the scaffold. Silas of Wickham and Thomas Galliard hurriedly moved toward the King and ordered the guards to take him to the noose.

But the arguing below became worse. "Hang him!" someone shouted.

"Set him free," others called back.

The mood was changing in the square. No longer was the crowd in agreement, no longer did they see the Green King as the criminal. And then it happened. Like the small trickle that leads to the bursting of the dam.

A voice called out in anger, "It's you who should be hanged!" But its charge was not aimed at the green figure on the scaffold but at the Abbot himself.

Whether it was from a townsman, who had been belittled by Guy de Bellambe, or from someone fed up with the high taxes to the abbey, it didn't matter. The fact was that it had been said. Suddenly, the crowd grew silent. They thought about who the real enemy was before them. The noble figure on the scaffold, or the conniving, power-hungry priest who presided over them all, with fear and contempt.

"It's you who should be hanged!" the voice shouted again, but this time it was not alone. Others called out in support, "Yes, Bellambe, you are the enemy of the weak and powerless. Give up some of your fine wines and rich food for the poor and the hungry!"

Wickham and Galliard sensed the danger. Slowly, they edged away from the scaffold and stood by the steps. The witchfinder stared coldly across at the King and his crown. He wanted it, and he wanted him executed, but there was no time now. He knew that at any moment, all hell would break loose.

"How dare you!" Bellambe strode to the edge of the scaffold and answered the jeers with his customary arrogance. "Get back to your hovels and let us deal with this witch and heretic."

"Perhaps it's time to let us deal with you!" the mob jeered back.

Then a burly townsman tried to climb the scaffold. He grabbed the wooden structure and with an almighty heave, he pulled himself up. Bellambe backed away and clicked his fingers.

The guard nearest him, pulled out a crossbow, quickly loaded a bolt and fired. The bolt struck the townsman in the shoulder; he stumbled and fell backward into the crowd below.

Cries and screams rang out and chaos took over. The crowd now rose as one, allied in their hatred of the Abbot and they stormed the scaffold. The abbey guards fired and their bolts flew, but there were too many of them and they were quickly overwhelmed.

The Abbot looked around for Silas and Galliard, but they had already fled. Then, the crowd were upon him and Bellambe suddenly found himself being hauled up above the heads of the crowd. With a cry of terror, his head was pushed through his own noose.

As confusion reigned upon the scaffold, Sir Richard and Cob Fletcher climbed up and cut the shackles that held the Green King captive. They pulled him away from the baying mob and off to safety, behind the abbey gates. Hickory helped Fern down from the statue and they hurriedly followed the others, whilst behind them the crowd cheered as the bishop was hanged!

Catching their breath in the shadows of the great gatehouse, Fern and Hickory found him at last. Their father, the man they had searched for all over England, the man they had missed so desperately, the man they loved.

Sir Richard and Cob stood by the entrance, checking no-one had followed them and as they drew away from the three green figures, the King looked down upon his children, who now stared back at him as if in a dream. There were no words said between them. That could wait until later. Now, in the midst of the mayhem all around them there was time only to hold each other for a few brief moments. They buried their heads in his chest and he held them tight.

"Tai mal armor," he whispered gently to them, "tai mal armor." Together at last!

But then the mob spilt out from the square and a line of abbey guards appeared. "Quick, to the horses," Cob cried. Fern gripped her father's hand and Hickory took the other and they all ran back to the Buttermarket before anyone tried to stop them. Within minutes, they rode away from Bury St Edmunds and left the town in turmoil behind them.

They were not the only ones to escape the chaos. If they had stayed two minutes longer by the abbey gates, they would have seen Silas of Wickham and Thomas Galliard crawl under the legs of the mob and slip away unseen through the backstreets of the town.

# 25. Reunited

*~ Together again, through wind and rain~*

"Thank you, for saving me," the Green King's voice was deep and resonant and it seemed to echo around the corners and beams of the great hall at *Wyken* Manor.

The dying sunlight streamed through the open windows and long shadows stretched across the stone floor like giant's fingers, as dusk began to fall. "Thank you also," he continued, "for bringing my children back to me."

The Green King was sat on a high backed wooden chair, a bandage was wrapped around his burnt hand and Fern and Hickory were sat at his feet. Indeed, Fern had not let go of her father's hand since they had rescued him. As for Hickory, he kept staring up at his father, just to check if he was really there with them.

"You are welcome, my friend," Sir Richard replied, "although, the one who has really taken care of these two over the last year, will not arrive until morning."

Sir Richard spoke of Nathaniel, who lay wounded on the cart that now brought him home to *Wyken*. Nathaniel, whose sight had been taken and who would never again see the soft pastures and ploughed fields of Suffolk.

"What do we call you?" Sir Richard poured the king a goblet of wine.

The King stared at the strange drink and then lifted the goblet to his lips. "My name is King Hylandus," he answered, wiping his chin with a grin, "though I notice how you call Clyssa and Hylasses by their English terms: Fern and Hickory."

"So what is your name in our tongue?" Sir Richard continued.

The Green King thought for a moment, "I am named after a hedge," he stated and then he laughed. "Well, it is a tree with berries really. In your words, my name is Elder. King Elder to be precise. I learnt your language, when I was a boy. My father thought we should know of your world," he paused in thought for a moment. "Even then we knew of the dangers that threatened the woods."

"So what happened to us Father?" Fern looked into King Elder's eyes and the King stared back at her.

"Yes," Sir Richard added, "how did you and the children come to be separated?"

"Let me start at the beginning." King Elder stared out through the great hall's window and far away to the trees on the horizon. "For many years, men have been encroaching on the wild forests. Wood has many uses. We of all people know that. But your people have come to realise it too. So we watch in hiding as great oaks are felled for ships, yews are taken to make your bows, willows for baskets, hazel for fences, the silver birch to make tools, the wide sycamore for your musical instruments, beautiful walnut for chairs and tables. The list is endless."

"We all have need for timber," Sir Richard answered trying to defend man's use of the woods.

"I understand that," King Elder said, "but now we find men cutting the trees down for other reasons. To create new farmland, to clear the woods for settlement, for towns, roads and farms."

"I see," Sir Richard replied thoughtfully.

"One day many men came. They cut down many trees. Piles of timber, mountains of chippings, all for ships we overheard them say, a navy to fight your wars on the shining sea. Then, some of the men saw us and we were forced to flee. We escaped and we climbed into the trees, but that was when we lost these two." He rested his hands on the shoulders of Fern and Hickory.

"They fell! I saw them crash to the ground but could do nothing. So I asked the birds to cover them with leaves. The men came and did not see the children." He paused for a moment. "But by the time I returned to rescue them, they were gone!"

"Cob Fletcher had found us," Fern stated, "but our memories were lost to us."

"A bang on the head can do that," Sir Richard said. "It explains your state when you were brought to me."

"Over time pieces of memory have returned, but then they are lost again," Fern reflected.

"You have been far away from your home and that has not helped you to reclaim your thoughts," Sir Richard added.

"But now it is all returning," Fern smiled and Hickory nodded. The presence of their father had brought their memories flooding back. Visions of their woodland home, the faces of their people, the happiness of their life in the trees, the sadness of the loss of their mother. All these memories and more raced through their minds now.

"But what will you return home to?" King Elder stated sadly. " Our homeland is being taken from us. The trees are vital to our existence. It is where we live; it is where we have lived for many years. Unseen by the world of men. All we need is in the trees, we want nothing more than to be left in peace."

"Then we must find a way to help you," Sir Richard stated. "I must go and talk with those that will listen."

"And who is that?" asked Fern.

"King Henry himself," Sir Richard replied. "I will go to London immediately."

"Will it do any good?" King Elder's face shone with hope.

"I cannot say, but the King is a good man and I am sure something can be done." Sir Richard rose from his chair and rang a bell to call a servant to pack for him. "You must stay here. Rest and recuperate. Walk through the orchards, catch up with talk of your home and tell your father of your adventures. And look after Nathaniel when he returns."

# 26. The Holly Crown
## ~ Holly holly, the sacred tree~

The following morning the army returned home. Sir Richard saw them in and was amazed to see Nathaniel sitting at the front of the cart that led the troops along the winding dirt track to Wyken Manor.

"Home, at last, Nathaniel." Sir Richard helped the old man down from the cart.

"Home at last," Nathaniel replied.

"You're here!" Hickory shouted as he ran to embrace the old man. "Wonderful news, Nat. Wonderful news. Father is here!"

"I am so glad, Hickory." The old man smiled and with Hickory taking one arm and Sir Richard taking the other, they guided Nathaniel into Wyken Manor.

❦❦❦

"I do not have the words to thank you enough." King Elder stood before Nathaniel and shook his hand.

"It was a pleasure to help," Nathaniel replied. "I have learnt so much from these two, that I feel like a child again."

"I can also see what you have gone through

and the sacrifice you have made for my children," the King's voice was deep and solemn. "I will not forget that, Nathaniel."

Once Sir Richard had greeted all his men back home, he rode off to London, hopeful of an audience with King Henry. "A week," he said, "I will be back within the week. Simeon will look after you all and try not to get into any more trouble!" He laughed and then kicked his spurs and rode away on his horse, Firefly.

"I must have it, Galliard. I must!" Silas of Wickham was pouring himself a goblet of wine, whilst Thomas Galliard sat smiling, in the upper chambers of the manor house at Wickham Market. "I am sure there is some power in it. Some devilish magic, which I can use to my own ends. I must have it!" he repeated.

"And you shall, my Lord," Galliard said smugly.

"But, how Thomas? How?" Wickham sat himself down on his chair

"By stealth, my Lord. By cunning and surprise!" Galliard replied. "We will enter Wyken Manor like foxes in a hen-house, with speed and guile. We will have your holly crown before anyone even knows we are there. And we may have time to take some revenge too!"

"And by what wizardry will you transport us unseen into the heart of *Wyken Manor?*" Wickham looked perturbed. "De Calne has plenty of guards and we are hardly welcome. He would kill me on sight and you are hardly flavour of the month, need I remind you!"

"I have a plan, my Lord." Galliard smiled.

"Then tell me more Thomas," Wickham grinned. "Tell me more!"

# 27. The Chronicles of Wyken
### ~ Inside the pages of a book is where the
### wise and curious look ~

During the following few days, Fern and Hickory showed King Elder the wonders of life in and around Wyken Manor. They took him to the watermill and the beehives. They led him to the kitchens, where Mary the Cook gave them all honeycakes. They visited churches and watched the harvest being brought in. Finally, they took him to Woolpit and introduced him to the Fletchers, and there they renewed their friendship with Till and Meg. And all the while the sun shone and their wounds mended.

One late afternoon, almost a week after Sir Richard had left for London, two figures moved slowly along the corridor at the top of the Manor house. Indeed, the smaller one led the other by the hand. The passageway was long and narrow and the wooden floorboards creaked underneath their feet. At times the taller figure put his hands out in front of him, feeling the way. Once or twice he stumbled, but the boy beside him, steadied him and they carried on until they stood in front of an oak door.

"I haven't been able to come up here, until now," Nathaniel stood outside his old chamber.

Since returning to the great house, he had taken a ground floor bedchamber for convenience. Walking blindly was hard enough, trying to get up stairs would only have complicated matters. But he was finding his feet now, and besides, Hickory was always there to help and support him.

But it wasn't the flight of stairs that had prevented the old man from coming up to his old room. It was the frustration of realising that all the treasures of knowledge inside his books were shut to him now. But Hickory was there and he turned the latch, opened the door and led Nathaniel inside.

The room was much unchanged since the last time the two of them had stood there, almost a year ago. The scrolls, manuscripts and books were still spilling out from the shelves. The wooden chests were full of relics, statues and weapons and there were bottles, potions and vials littered on the tables and desks.

Hickory ushered his old friend over to a wooden chair and sat him down upon it. Then Hickory ran outside, nipped down the corridor and grabbed a book from his own room. Within seconds, he was back in the chamber again, before Nathaniel had even realised he'd left him alone.

"Try this," Hickory smiled and he put the book down on the desk before Nathaniel.

"Hickory, I can't see a thing. Don't tease me boy!" The old man laid his hand on the book and pushed it away.

"I know that, Nathaniel. But this book is special. I have made it for you!" Hickory pushed the book back again and opened it up on the first page. "Read with your fingers, Nathaniel. Read with your fingers."

"What are you talking about, boy? How exactly do I read with my fingers?"

"Here," Hickory replied, "let me show you." Very slowly, Hickory put the old man's bony old finger on the page. Nathaniel then searched around for a few minutes and suddenly found something slightly raised on the parchment. The old man moved his finger and followed the shape of the lines and then he smiled. "It's a letter!" he said.

"Can you work out which one it is?" Hickory asked.

"Nathaniel's finger moved again. "It's an F," he answered excitedly.

"Correct!" Hickory grinned. "Now try the whole line."

Nathaniel traced his finger along the row of risen letters and then laughed. "Fern's potion for sore feet!"

"That's right," Hickory's face beamed.

"But this is marvellous, Hickory. How have

you done it?" Nathaniel moved his finger off the page.

"I have written the words using candle wax." Hickory explained. "It took a while to work out how to do it and it takes ages to drop the wax in a line. I used one of your glass vials, which helped it to fall in a thin dribble, and it seemed to work."

"It's ingenious," Nathaniel stated, "but there is something I don't understand, Hickory. You can't even read!"

"Simeon has been teaching me these last few days," the boy replied with pride. "If I am to be of any use to you, then I need to read. But I will not always be here, not now that Father has been found, so I tried to think of a way I could help you get your eyes back. At least with regard to reading."

"It's wonderful Hickory!" The old man was almost lost for words. "Reading with my fingers. Who could have thought it possible?"

"Anything is possible Nat," Hickory laughed. "Anything is possible!"

"So it seems!" The old man reached out his arm and ruffled the boy's hair. "Thank you Hickory, thank you."

He did not of course see his young friend wipe away the tears from his cheeks. *A little of what I owe him has been repaid*, Hickory thought. *A little!*

☙❦☙❦☙

An hour later, Hickory was practising his reading, whilst Nathaniel listened, half-asleep in his chair.

'The Danes then invaded, with a fleet of great ships. They quickly captured many towns and villages in East Anglia. Eventually, King Edmund was taken and the Danes tied him to a tree and shot him with arrows. Then, the brave King was beheaded and his head was thrown into thickets. When later his followers tried to find his remains, they found the head guarded by a wolf and the head was calling here, here, here. So at last his whole remains could be buried.'

Hickory stopped reading and closed the book with a thump. "Very good, lad," Nathaniel awoke with a start.

"So is that how Bury St Edmunds got its name?" Hickory asked.

"It is indeed," Nathaniel replied.

"You have so many books here," Hickory replaced the story of Saint Edmund and was amazed by the rows of leather-bound volumes before him. "But there's a gap here, Nathaniel," Hickory noticed a space in one of the shelves.

"What books are either side?" Nathaniel

asked.

"A book about the creatures of the Far East and a book on the Coasts of France. What should have been in the middle?"

Normally the old man knew, but he hadn't been here for a year. He thought for a moment longer and then said, "I can't quite remember."

"Here it is," said Thomas Galliard. " I stole this from old Drinkstone's library. A book of the secrets of Suffolk." The two men were still plotting in the witchfinder's chamber at Wickham Market.

"And what use is this!" Silas of Wickham replied angrily, grabbing the leather-bound volume from Galliard.

"Look at page twelve, my Lord." Galliard moved away from Wickham and watched in silence as the witchfinder thumbed through the book.

Silas hurriedly found the page and read softly to himself. His voice hissed like a snake and from the other side of the room, Galliard thought how fortunate he was that Wickham wasn't his enemy. A sly smile came over the witchfinder's face. "I see," he said, "well done, Thomas. Well done indeed!"

"Thank you, my Lord." Galliard replied.

"A secret tunnel in *Wyken Manor*." Wickham closed the book and moved quickly to the door of the chamber. "Who would have thought it!"

# 28. Night Attack
## ~ Evil treads softly~

A flurry of hooves thundered on the stone track that led up the hill toward the small hamlet of Badwell, as the two horsemen rode fast through the night. Quickly, they passed by the sleeping village, left the track and struck out across the open meadows.

By the time they appeared on the edge of the estate of Wyken Manor it had turned well past midnight. The two riders tethered their horses to an old oak tree and silently they strode toward the manor house. A silver half-moon appeared from behind the high clouds and the men became silhouettes in the crisp night air.

"What does the book show?" the first horseman asked and turned to face his companion.

"The opening is over there by that old stone barn," the second rider replied, and pointed to the half-ruined shack that lay before them.

"Come on then," whispered the first rider, "let's get moving!" Silently and swiftly the two men pushed open the wooden doors of the ancient barn and slipped inside.

Inside Wyken Manor, the whole household lay sound asleep. The servants had finished their duties and had retired to their quarters long ago. Nathaniel and Simeon lay asleep in their chambers in the west wing of the manor house and Fern, King Elder and Hickory slumbered away in their rooms in the east wing. And the one guard that was to remain on duty through the night, sat half-asleep on a bench by the front door. So as the tiny wooden trapdoor opened in the corner of the great hall, nobody heard a thing.

A pair of eyes peered out from the dark hole, they scanned the torch-lit hall, and then the door was slowly pushed upward. Silently, two men climbed out and, hurriedly replacing the door, they stood against the wall and hid in the shadows.

"I know my way around here like the back of my hand." Thomas Galliard, once steward of the manor, now cast his eyes around his old employer's home.

"So which way do we go?" Silas of Wickham whispered.

"The King will be in the guest quarters, in the east wing," Galliard replied. "Follow me."

And the two dark figures crept along the corridors of the sleeping manor house.

Hickory's eyes opened. He sensed danger. Something or someone was in the house, he was sure of it. He lay quite still in his bed and listened to the sounds of the night.

Outside his window, he could just make out the faint call of a fox. But that was some miles off. It was inside the house where he heard the noises. The sound of oak floorboards creaking. The soft but certain tread of riding boots on the stone floor of the great hall. With a jump he hopped out of bed and stood silently by his bedroom door.

Slowly, he turned the handle, inched the door open and put his ear to the gap. Footsteps! He was sure of it. Too loud to be Fern or his father and unlikely to be a servant at this time of night, he thought. Carefully, he pushed the door open wide and slipped outside into the open corridor.

In the flickering light of the wall-torches Hickory stood motionless, frozen against the timbered wall of the hallway, as two figures moved toward the door of his father's room. Then, he watched in fear, as one by one they entered the bedchamber.

Hickory followed them to the doorway and peered inside, just in time to see the first figure grab King Elder's holly crown from the desk, in the corner of the room. The boy's sharp eyes then spotted the other figure, who stood silently over the sleeping form of his father. The figure drew a knife from his belt and raised his arm into the air, above the King's chest.

"No!" Hickory screamed and he ran, head down, at the black robed figure.

His charge knocked the knife from the attacker's hand and his cry of alarm awoke King Elder. Confusion now reigned. The attacker was winded by Hickory's charge and he stumbled backward against the bed, whilst Hickory himself landed on the floor with a thump.

The Green King quickly took in what was happening and tried to grab hold of his assailant, but somehow he wriggled free of the King's grasp.

Meanwhile, the other figure, who'd snatched the holly crown, was already running out of the door. His accomplice now jumped over Hickory and followed in pursuit. "Wait, Silas!" he shouted. But the witchfinder had already disappeared down the corridor to find the opening of the secret tunnel.

With all the noise, half of Wyken Manor was now awake. By the time Fern and Simeon appeared, in the hallway, a liveried guard was ringing the alarm bell.

"What's happening?" Simeon shouted as Hickory and King Elder followed Galliard to the great hall.

"Intruders!" the King replied on the run.

"Silas of Wickham and your old steward," Hickory added. "They've stolen Father's crown."

Fern and Simeon now joined the chase and as all four of them entered the great hall, they just caught a glimpse of Galliard's robes disappearing down the secret tunnel's entrance.

"Well, I never," Simeon gasped in surprise.

"Come on. Let's get after them," Hickory cried and they all jumped into the blackness below!

# 29. Tunnels and Trees

*~ Delve deep, into the ground, into the darkness*
*where the shadows are found ~*

Underneath the halls of Wyken Manor, Silas of Wickham and Thomas Galliard ran for their lives. But now they found the going difficult. They had no torch to light their way and at least twice, they both stumbled on loose stones. Then, at a particularly sharp corner Galliard's robe became ensnared in the rock face. "Silas, help me," he squealed, as he tugged at the robe.

The witchfinder turned and stared at his co-conspirator. He weighed up the options in his head. If he left Galliard to their pursuers they might not bother chasing him. Besides, it looked like it would take time to cut him free. Time he didn't have. He could already hear the footsteps coming this way.

"Sorry, Thomas," he cackled and away he fled.

"Damn you!" Galliard's screams followed the witchfinder down the black tunnel.

There was only one thing left to do. Galliard pushed himself back against the wall and covered himself with his black robe. He drew in his breath and stood as still as he could.

The first pursuers to come past him were

Hickory and King Elder. They moved so fast that Galliard barely noticed they had gone past. But their speed meant that they had missed him in his hiding place. He breathed out with a sigh of relief at his narrow escape.

But as he did so, Fern suddenly approached. "I can see you," she stated. "Come out from there."

"Certainly, my Lady." Galliard unmasked himself and stepped out from the gloom like a phantom. Then, he drew his dagger and smiled at Fern. "And what exactly do you think you are going to do now?" he sniggered.

"Clamp you in chains, and let my father deal with you!" To Galliard's surprise it was not Fern who answered him, but Simeon de Calne, who had appeared at her shoulder.

"You run on to the others," Simeon instructed. "I'll deal with him!"

Fern smiled back at him and she ran after her father and brother.

"So the young master has become a man, I see," Galliard sneered through the darkness.

"Out of your clutches, yes!" Simeon replied with defiance toward his old mentor and the two of them stood in the tunnel, eyeing one another, like stags ready to fight.

"Your father's son, at last," Galliard edged to the side of the tunnel, and back into the dark shadows. "So all's well that ends well. Yet, I had such high hopes for you, Simeon."

"You just wanted to use me to gain power for yourself at Wyken Manor," Simeon responded.

"Quite so, Simeon," Galliard replied, "and it nearly worked, too. Never mind! I'll just have to settle on revenge instead." With that, he lunged out through the darkness and stabbed his dagger toward him.

Simeon caught sight of the glint of steel at the last minute. He twisted his body away from the attack and moved just in time. The blade only nicked his shoulder and though he winced with the pain, he now had time to strike back. He moved much faster than his old mentor. He grabbed Galliard's wrist and smashed his hand against the tunnel wall.

Galliard cried out and the dagger fell from his grasp. They struggled for a few moments, before Simeon finally overpowered him. Then, he felt around in the gloom for the dagger, picked it up and held the blade to Galliard's throat.

"Go on then! Kill me! That's what you want to do, Simeon. I can see it in your eyes. You still have that cold, cruel streak in you. I know it!" Galliard grinned.

Simeon felt sorely tempted. Galliard's betrayal deserved punishment and the young man's anger rose, but he knew it was not the right thing to do. He held his emotions in check and lowered his hand.

"What a shame!" Galliard sneered. "You have grown up indeed, young master. The old Simeon would have exacted his revenge with glee!"

"Revenge is not a good emotion, Thomas," Simeon responded calmly.

Galliard let out a bitter laugh, "You sound just like your father. Noble and self-righteous - how sad!"

"Actually, that pleases me greatly, Thomas. I will take it as a compliment," Simeon smiled. Then, two manor guards suddenly appeared behind him and Simeon turned to meet them. "Take him away," he ordered.

The guards gripped Galliard by the shoulders, only too glad to have their mean old steward in their hands. Galliard glared coldly back at Simeon, but he had no more venom in him and the guards pulled him down the tunnel and off toward the cells.

So Galliard was captured. Simeon looked ahead, down the dark tunnel, and realised he had lost Wickham's trail. Would Fern, Hickory and King Elder be able to catch up with the witchfinder? And if they did, could they stop him? There was no time to waste. Simeon ran on into the darkness!

Silas gasped for air as he reached the opening of the tunnel. Hurriedly, he hauled himself out of the black hole and ran toward the barn door. The holly crown was gripped tightly in his left hand, whilst he drew his long bladed dagger with his right. Then, he stopped for a moment by the doorway. Should he wait and attack the green devils when they appeared from the tunnel, or should he make a run for it?

An owl hooted in the rafters above and startled him. He decided to run. He pushed open the barn doors and sprinted to where the horses were tethered. But when he got there, the horses were gone. He swore loudly and lashed out at the air around him. Then, he turned behind him. There were voices coming from the trees.

Wickham edged forward and peered into the woods and there, in an open glade, he saw two children, crouching down where they appeared to be feeding something. He was about to leave them to it, but then, the doors of the barn were pushed open again and racing toward him came the green devils.

The green boy held a long stick in his hand and he came toward the witchfinder with a fearless look. The girl too, showed no fear as she followed her brother out from the barn. Wickham suddenly panicked. He ran into the glade where the two children were and grabbed the first child by the scruff of the neck.

"Get off me!" Meg Fletcher screamed. But Silas took his dagger to her throat and edged her over to a clump of trees. Till, the other child in the glade, scampered out of the way. And then, with his back against a large oak tree, Silas stared out defiantly as Fern, Hickory and Till now encircled him.

"Come any closer and I'll snap her pretty neck!" he hissed.

"What do you want from us?" Fern's voice shook with a mixture of fear and anger.

"I have what I want right here," Wickham gestured at the holly crown, that was hanging from his belt. "Although, your execution in a sea of flames would be a bonus!" he cackled.

"Just let her go, and you can leave!" Fern answered his scornful plea. "You can keep the crown, though it won't be of any use to you. It must be worn by one who has a good heart."

Silas laughed. "Well, you are so gracious, my green lady!" He moved further back and rested himself against the trunk of the oak.

Then, another figure stepped out of the shadows. "Do as my daughter says. Move away

from the girl!" King Elder's voice was deep and solemn and it startled Wickham, as he appeared behind the witchfinder.

"I would not trust a green monster like you, if my life depended upon it." His eyes narrowed and he gripped tight on his dagger and drew it near to his hostage. The blade nipped Meg's skin and she winced. "Now, get down on your knees, all of you!" Silas screamed.

The King's face took on a sad demeanour. "So be it," he said, "there is no other way." And then, his voice boomed out across the glade and the leaves on the trees shook in reverence. "Calar tai morthrund," he bellowed. "Calar tai morthrund!"

Suddenly, the branches of the oak tree behind Wickham, came to life. Long tendrils wrapped themselves around the witchfinder and Silas screamed. His dagger fell to the floor and he let loose his grip of Meg. She pushed away his arm, slipped from his grasp and ran into Fern's arms.

Then, the branches squeezed tight. Silas clawed at them, but his squirming only made things worse. His face contorted and his eyes bulged as the branches strengthened their grip. One limb then slipped around his throat. It began to choke him and then moments later, he gasped his final breath.

The children and the King watched in awe as the oak tree released its grip and Silas of Wickham fell limply to the grassy floor. No more would he persecute the old and the weak, no more would he torture and execute the innocent!

Fern and Hickory stared at the face of the man who had chased them through Suffolk. The man that had wanted to burn them as witches. "It is over!" Fern said at last. She turned to the Fletchers and smiled. "What were you two doing out here at this time of night anyway?" Fern asked the twins.

"Feeding your rabbits!" grinned Till.

"Since you set them free from the Abbot's warren last year, they have run wild," Meg added. "If we don't come up here and feed them, they eat all our vegetables. It makes father mad!"

They all laughed and then Simeon appeared.

"Better late than never," Hickory grinned as Simeon entered the glade.

"I can't always save you Pignut!" Simeon answered back. "But I am glad you are all safe. Galliard is in the cells, so we should all sleep soundly in our beds tonight!"

"Come on then, let us return to Wyken Manor." King Elder picked up the holly crown from the floor by the oak tree. He patted the trunk in thanks, and they all made to leave the glade.

"But what about him?" Till pointed down at the dead body of the witchfinder.

"Leave him to the forest," King Elder replied. "He will be gone by morning."

"Come on then," Simeon smiled, "I don't know what I'll tell Father. I was supposed to be looking after you all."

Hickory slapped him on the back and laughed.

"No hunting or honeycakes, for a month," he chuckled and Simeon chased him back to the manor.

# 30. The Treaty of the Trees
## ~ Simple men argue, wise men agree ~

"I have returned with good news!" Sir Richard grinned as he entered the great hall and took off his cloak.

"Well, what is it?" Hickory asked, moving his counter to beat his father at chequers.

"Yes, tell us all about it," Nathaniel added. He was stood with Fern behind Hickory and King Elder and they were listening to Simeon play a new tune on his rebec.

"Well, while all you lot have been sitting around playing, I have had an audience with the King himself," Sir Richard smiled. He had heard of Wickham's plot and the witchfinder's demise, but he couldn't resist teasing them.

"We have not been sitting around!" Fern exclaimed.

"I know," Sir Richard replied, "I have heard of what happened and I am glad to return to find you all safe."

"Enough of that," Hickory cried, "what did the King say?"

"Patience, Son," King Elder stretched out a hand and placed it on Hickory's shoulder. "You must learn to wait for others."

"Yes, Father," Hickory smiled.

"Why don't you all come and see what I have got." Sir Richard reached into his saddlebag and pulled out a ribbon-bound document.

"What is that?" Fern asked, moving toward the great oak table where Sir Richard now stretched out the parchment.

"It's an agreement," he answered her and then began to read it out to them all.

---

**Settlement of land rights between King Henry of England and King Elder of the Greenwood**

I, Henry of England, hereby declare that the woods of East Anglia are the sole property of the Green People. Under the rule of King Elder, these lands are now forbidden to the English. The King and his people shall remain in peace and harmony, for as long as they desire.

Henry Plantagenet, King of England

---

King Elder studied the document more closely and read it again. Hickory followed his father and though he stumbled over one or two words he managed to read it through to the end.

"Well, your Majesty," Sir Richard looked King Elder in the face, "what do you say?"

The King stood silently for a moment. He stared down at the document and closed his eyes as if deep in thought. Then, he opened them and smiled. "I am in agreement," he laughed. "It is better than I could have hoped for Sir Richard. Thank you on behalf of all my people."

They all cheered and Simeon played a merry tune as Hickory and Fern danced arm in arm, whilst their father signed the Treaty of the Trees.

⚜⚜⚜

With the threat of Silas of Wickham gone and the harsh rule of the Abbot at an end, Suffolk seemed to thrive in the summer that followed.

The wheat was as tall as anyone could remember, the vegetables were huge and the fruit hung heavy on the trees. It seemed to many that the sun did not stop shining for weeks on end, and the sound of laughter rang merrily throughout the farms and villages surrounding Wyken Manor.

And then something else occurred. Something wonderful, and quite unexpected! Romance blossomed, between Fern and Simeon.

No one knew how it happened, not even Fern and Simeon. A smile, a gentle word at mealtimes, a brushing of shoulders as they passed in the corridor. But happen it did!

There followed quiet horse rides together over the green meadows, paddling in the millstream, long walks through the fields of golden corn and hours spent staring up at the wide Suffolk skies.

So, perhaps it was no surprise to anyone, when Simeon finally plucked up courage to ask King Elder, for Fern's hand in marriage.

"She is very dear to us, Simeon," the Green King stated softly. "And we are few and you are many. To lose her again so soon, would break my heart."

Simeon looked downcast and the King saw his gloomy demeanour. "I did not say no, Simeon. I just ask that you wait a while. That is all."

"How long?" Simeon asked, smiling again.

"A year," the King said. "A year from today. We will return next summer. And if your feelings for each other are still the same, then it shall be so."

Simeon grinned. "Thank you, your Majesty. Thank you."

# 31. Faces in the Leaves
### ~ Behind the trees, deep in the wood, live a people with hearts that are wise and good ~

Toward the end of September, Fern, Hickory and King Elder received news. Though it was an unlikely messenger that arrived in the great hall, one Sunday evening.

The robin that bobbed about on the windowsill chirped away merrily and then stretched its tiny wings and flew off again, into the sunset.

"Well, what was all that about?" Sir Richard looked at his green friends in bafflement.

"They are coming," King Elder replied thoughtfully.

"Who are coming?" Nathaniel asked, sitting up in his chair.

"Our people," Hickory took hold of the old man's hand. "Our people, Nathaniel."

"When will they be here?" Simeon looked anxious. He knew that meant Fern would soon be leaving.

"Tomorrow, Simeon," Fern answered him. "In the morning we will leave." She strode over to him and kissed him lightly on the cheek. "But we will return," she smiled. "I will return."

So it was the following morning as they all approached the woods behind the wolfpits that a familiar melody drifted through the trees. At first, it sounded as if the wind itself was singing the words, so light and gentle was the sound, but then the voices became clearer and stronger.

## The Song of the Green King

*The Lord of all the Greenwood, the Guardian of the trees.*
*The King of Golden Summer, in his land within the leaves.*

*The green forest is his home,*
*And his Kingdom now is growing*
*There he'll take you by the hand*
*to the waters that are flowing.*

*The Lord of all the Greenwood, the Guardian of the trees.*
*The King of Golden Summer, in his land within the leaves.*

*Yes, his power can still be found,*
*behind every branch and leaf.*
Our Green King has again been found
and will save us all from grief.

The Lord of all the Greenwood, the Guardian of the trees.
The King of Golden Summer, in his land within the leaves.

Then, out from the bushes and the hedges, pushing back long-stemmed plants and brushing past leaf-clad branches, the woodland people emerged from the trees.

Dressed in a dozen shades of green they came. The women, garlanded with flowers and the men carrying wooden staffs. Their hair was pale and their skin was green and upon their faces, smiles beamed wide and their voices were light and merry.

As they appeared through the half-light, Fern smiled and then she recited their names to Simeon, instantly translating them as each one of her people passed into view. "That's Woodbine and Briar," she stated, when two large green men stepped out from the shadows. "And Foxglove and Willowherb," she continued, when two tall slender women joined the men.

"And who are they?" Simeon asked, whilst he pointed at the three young girls, who had just skipped into the clearing.

"That's Snowdrop, Crocus and Buttercup," Fern answered with a laugh.

Others now followed them out from the depths of the woods. Three tall, proud looking, young men, that Fern named as Bitterbark, Chestnut and Cedar. Two older women, wise and thoughtful, they looked, grey-eyed and grey-haired. "Whitebeam and Larch," Fern whispered, "great healers, who make my knowledge of plants seem feeble."

"I doubt that," replied Simeon and Fern blushed.

Virtually tumbling out from the undergrowth came a noisy gang of unkempt boys. Bark, Ragweed, Bramble and Mulberry they were called, though they rarely stood still long enough to answer. They ran over to Hickory and began to push and shove each other, whilst they asked him all about his adventures.

Fern laughed at the boys, and then she looked upon her brother with fresh eyes. She had never thought of him as someone that people would look up to, but she had begun to realise that one day, of course, he would be king.

Lastly, came an old white-haired man that reminded them of Nathaniel. Elm was his name and a wise and trusted counsellor to the King he had been. He strode over to King Elder and bowed before him.

"Welcome back my Lord," he said.

"Thank you, Elm. It is good to be back. And I bring good news too." Elder gave the old counsellor King Henry's treaty and as he read it, the old man smiled.

"Well," Sir Richard said, "it is good to meet you all." The woodland people swarmed around the party. They shook hands with Sir Richard,

Simeon and Cob Fletcher. They patted Meg and Till on the head and many of them hugged Nathaniel. They were so pleased to see their King and the children returned to them.

"We are thankful to you all," Elm spoke in a clear, crisp voice that belied his years. "It was hard enough to lose the children, but when Elder went missing, we thought all hope was lost. Yet, now you are all safe, we have the freedom of the woods and you are returning home with us."

"Only for a while," Fern spoke softly. "I am to return in a year." She caught Simeon's gaze and held it for a moment. He smiled in return.

"What's this?" Elm asked.

"Fern and Simeon are to be wed next summer," King Elder explained.

Some of the green people clapped, others came and kissed Fern and shook Simeon's hand vigorously. Though some also looked sad, for they knew Fern would be leaving them, once again.

"Until next summer, then," Sir Richard took the King's hand and shook it and as the sun dipped, the two men stood together, tall and strong and noble.

Realising they were leaving, Hickory ran over to Nathaniel and hugged the old man. "I will be back," he said gently. "I cannot say how sorry I am."

Nathaniel put his hand on his young

friend's shoulder. "I know lad, I do not hold you to any blame. I chose to take the path we took. Now, do not worry, Sir Richard and Simeon will take good care of me."

Slipping away from the crowd, Fern and Simeon stood under the caress of an old chestnut tree. "A year seems like an eternity right now," Simeon clasped Fern's hand tightly.

"It will soon pass," Fern touched his cheek and looked into his eyes, "when next summer comes, look to the woods. I will send you messages and then we will be together." She kissed him and they embraced.

Watching the two of them from the crowd, Meg smiled and the green girls Fern had named as Snowdrop, Crocus and Buttercup, giggled.

Then, as quickly and as quietly as they had appeared from the trees, the woodland people slipped away again. Though, this time they took with them three of their own.

# 32. Fern and Simeon

~ *When bound together, we live forever...*
*in each other's hearts* ~

It was a beautiful summer's morning when the procession appeared on the edge of Nunty's Wood. Merrily, it wove its way through the cornfields and the long lines of vegetables and then it turned down toward the village of Woolpit.

Leading the way was Hickory, he had grown six inches over the last twelve months and somehow looked wiser and nearer manhood, though there was still a boyish twinkle in his eye. He was dressed in a fine tunic of emerald green and he wore a circlet of holly on his head.

Behind him came many of the woodland folk, all dressed in beautiful shades of green. They sang as they walked and their soft voices filled the air like birdsong.

At the back of the procession came the King. He had a fine green robe around his shoulders that shimmered like falling leaves. Next to him was Fern. She was dressed in a long flowing white gown that sparkled in the sunlight. She wore a garland of daisies upon her brow and she carried a posy of wildflowers in her hand.

As they approached the church, Meg

Fletcher appeared from behind the lych-gate. She smiled at Fern and lifting her bridesmaid's gown she ran over to her, slipped behind her in the procession and followed her into the church.

Inside, the pews were full. For all the villagers that had come to know the green children from their time with them last year had turned out to see the celebration. Cob and Martha Fletcher were there. Till and Bull Weaver, now firm friends, stood grinning together at the back. Will Middlefoot the reeve, Tam One-eye, Gan the Swineherd, Barnet the Miller and many others were all crammed into the tiny church. Then the woodland folk entered and took their places, mingling freely with the villagers.

In the front pew sat Sir Richard and Nathaniel. And in front of the altar stood Simeon. He was dressed in a clear blue surcoat and the white ship of the de Calne coat of arms was emblazoned on his chest. Then, Hickory came down to join him and he stood next to Simeon, for he was to be his best man.

"Do you have it?" Simeon whispered as Hickory winked at him.

Hickory suddenly raised his eyebrows and feigned concern. "Have what?" he grinned. "Don't you dare, Pignut!" Simeon glared.

Hickory laughed and handed him a tiny wooden box. Simeon carefully opened it and took out a beautiful ring.

"It's carved from the wood of the cherry tree, for the cherry is the tree of the heart," Hickory stated knowledgably. "It was worn by our mother and now it will be worn by Fern."

"And what is the stone?" Simeon asked, staring at the honey coloured gem.

"It's not a stone," Hickory answered, "it's amber. The fossilised sap of a tree. Now, turn and face your bride."

Simeon looked behind him and then he saw her. He wondered if he had seen anything so beautiful before. It was not just the beauty of her face or the dress that shimmered in the sunlight, but it was her shining spirit and her tender heart. And when Fern walked down the aisle to meet him, everyone inside the church held their breath.

She reached the altar, turned and smiled at Simeon and then she took her place beside him, whilst King Elder and Meg Fletcher stood behind them. Then, in a clear voice, Brother Cuthbert read the vows and the church listened in silence.

Once the ceremony was over, Simeon placed the ring on Fern's finger and the guests inside the church cheered. Then, they made their way outside and as they strolled out under the lychgate, the children of Woolpit threw rose petals over the newlyweds.

All the villagers and the woodland people then followed the two of them up the hill, past

the cornfields and onto the feast that lay spread out under the eaves of the trees by Nunty's Wood. And it was not long before they were all sat down, and the food and wine were flowing.

Once everyone had eaten their fill, they all sat back to listen to the speeches. "Days like these are sadly few and far between," Sir Richard stood up first, and addressed the wedding party. "To feel the sun on our faces, to have food in our bellies and to have hope in our hearts is a joyous thing!" The crowd cheered and Sir Richard bowed to them. Then, he turned to Fern and looked across to Hickory and nodded his head to King Elder. "Part of that good feeling is down to our new woodland friends. So I give you all a toast. 'To the Green People of the Woods!'" All the villagers and the household of Wyken Manor rose and drank.

King Elder now stood and he praised the feast and gave thanks to Sir Richard and his people. "Our bond is joined forever now, and who knows, perhaps one day we will even hear the pattering of tiny feet?" Everyone laughed and Fern and Simeon blushed. "I wonder what colour they will be?" King Elder mused and they all chuckled again. "So," the King continued, "raise your tankards to the happy couple. I give you Fern and Simeon."

Everyone now stood, they drank again and

then they put down their tankards and clapped their hands. Simeon and Fern stood up, hand-in-hand, and bowed before them all.

After that everyone followed Fern and Simeon to a trestle table, where there sat a vast array of wedding presents. As the couple opened each one, there was a chorus of cheers and gasps of wonder, for some of the presents were wondrous indeed.

One of the first gifts Fern opened was from Bishop Hugh of Lincoln. Everyone was very impressed that she had such eminent friends, but it was Hickory who laughed loudest as Fern opened up a stone statue of the Lincoln Imp. "Does it fly?" he grinned as he told Nathaniel what Fern had been given.

Other gifts were just as marvellous. There was a beautifully carved longbow - a present for Simeon, from a certain Robin Hood. Packaged in a wooden crate, was a tray of strange looking pastries. 'A gift from Cornwall', the scroll that accompanied the gift stated, 'from Ethan and William d'Vert'.

"What is it?" Hickory enquired.

"Some kind of pie," Simeon answered.

"I believe it's called a pasty," Nathaniel told them all.

"One half is savoury - cheese or meat, perhaps. The other end is sweet - fruit or honey."

"Wow!" Till grinned. "A whole meal in one!"

"Precisely," Nathaniel added, "I understand that they eat it down the tin-mines."

"What would we do without you?" Sir Richard patted his old friend on the back, as Till and Hickory tucked in to the pasties.

"Wonderful!" they both replied, wiping away the crumbs.

Just when they thought that they had seen everything, two figures appeared through the trees. The first one came forward, grinned a ragged-toothed smile and pushed his unkempt hair out of his face. He grunted a hello to Fern and handed her a large seashell. The crowd were amazed to see the wild man of Orford before their very eyes, but they made him welcome and he sat down with them.

He grunted again and pointed at the shell. "I think he wants you to open it," Simeon told her. Everyone gathered around and Fern opened the shell. They all gasped as they spied the beautiful gleaming white pearl that sat inside the oyster shell. Fern kissed the wild man on the cheek and they all laughed as he got up and danced a merry jig.

The other stranger now moved out from the shadows. He twirled his long-tailed coat when he strolled toward them all and he began to juggle some apples that he'd swiped from the feasting table.

"Harlequin!" smiled Fern.

"Well, my Lady," he bowed extravagantly toward her and winked over at Hickory. "You have come far, since first we met. No longer are you two frightened green children, but instead I see a fairy princess and a stout woodland prince."

"We never had a chance to thank you properly, back at Orford," Fern told him.

"I need no thanks," he replied. "My reward was knowing that we had outsmarted that awful constable and that wicked witchfinder. Whatever happened to him, by the way?"

Fern and Hickory glanced toward the forest.

"He is gone!" Hickory replied. "Good riddance, I say!" Then, he pulled out a flute and played a merry tune. His old magic had not deserted him and before long all the guests were up and dancing in and out of the trees.

And so the celebrations went on well into the night. But at one moment, late in the evening, Fern and Hickory caught each other's eye across the laughter and the music and the chatting and the cheering. In that moment they shared an instant of pure happiness.

It had been two years almost to the day, that Cob Fletcher had found them in the glade where they now sat. They turned away from each other and looked at the faces of the friends and family that now surrounded them, and they knew that their adventure had finally come to an end.

# 33. Bittersweet

*~ For every ray of sun, there is a drop of rain ~*

A cold crisp air rippled around the outhouses, barns and buildings of Wyken Manor.

Swallows gathered on the rooftops, making their plans to fly to warmer lands, blackberries ripened in the hedgerows and the leaves in the apple orchard began to fall.

Out in the fields, the plough teams strode across the farmlands of Wyken Manor with purpose, and the rich Suffolk soil was turned over and over and over. Within a few days the golden fields of corn had disappeared and were now exchanged for ploughed furrows of black earth.

And so it was, that summer slipped quietly into autumn, and one day, toward the middle of September, a small gathering could be seen up by Nunty's Wood.

"The time has come to leave," King Elder spoke quietly.

All those close by had known this day would come, but when it had finally arrived, it saddened them all.

Yet, the King and his people said their goodbyes to their new friends and then Elder shook Sir Richard's hand.

"We are bound together now and I am sure

we will meet again," he stated.

"We are bonded by family ties indeed," Sir Richard replied.

While the older ones found the parting difficult, it was much harder still for others to let go. No one saw Hickory say his goodbyes to Till, Meg and Fern for they strode one last time through the fields near the wolfpits, where they had first become friends.

After a while, Meg and Till pulled away and left Fern and Hickory alone. They spoke of their adventures together and the hardships they had gone through. They talked of the past and of what they hoped the future would bring and then they returned up to the woods.

"It is time," Nathaniel spoke softly to Hickory and the boy turned to his old companion with tears in his eyes. "Come with me," Hickory pleaded.

"But Wyken is my home, Hickory," the old man replied. "Without my sight, I need somewhere I am familiar with, somewhere I know and trust."

"Trust me," said Hickory, "I will show you the wonders of the forest. Deep inside, in the dark depths, you do not need eyes, Nathaniel. Just instinct!"

The old man pondered for a moment. "But what would Sir Richard do without me?" he grinned.

"True," Sir Richard smiled, "it would be so hard to run *Wyken Manor* without some grumbling old man."

Nathaniel stroked his beard and chuckled. "Very well then, lad. I will follow you into the wildwood again. One last journey, perhaps."

"So let me get this right," Sir Richard addressed the small gathering, "Fern comes to us and Nathaniel goes with you. I think we have the better of the bargain. Though in truth, I will miss our fireside chats and our games of chequers." Sir Richard looked away and if it weren't for the fact that he was a brave and noble knight, people who saw him would have said that he had a tear in his eye.

"Do you need anything Nathaniel?" he took his old friend's hand in his own.

"No, Sir Richard," the old man smiled, "just my staff and my cloak. It was ever so. I have journeyed far and wide and they are all I have seemed to really have had need of."

"Goodbye, then Nathaniel," Fern's voice was as soft and as sad as the robin's lonely winter tune.

"Well, girl," Nathaniel took Fern's slender hand in his grasp. Tears were streaming down the girl's face now. "We have come far, you and I," he told her.

"I will not forget you, Nathaniel," Fern whispered.

"Nor I you," he answered. Then he kissed her forehead and Fern passed his hand into Hickory's firm grip.

Then, Fern flung her arms around her father's neck.

"Remember," he whispered into her ear, "we are but a swallow's song away. When you are missing us, just look to the trees, Fern. Look to the trees."

Then, King Elder let her go. He put his hand on Hickory's shoulder and the King and the boy led Nathaniel and the woodland people to the trees. When they reached them they turned back to wave. Moments later, they were gone.

Fern stood a while, staring into the trees, listening to the birds sing and then Simeon gently took her hand. She turned around and smiled at him.

" Well, husband," she grinned, "let's go home!"

# At the End of Days...

A few months after their wedding day it was said that Fern and Simeon went north, to live in a beautiful timbered manor house on the de Calne lands near King's Lynn in Norfolk. As the years passed gently away, Fern's green colour faded a little and when she had children of her own they were as pale in complexion as any other child.

Here, she lived in comfort and kindness for a great number of years. She continued with her love of plants and her knowledge of the healing powers of herbs made her famous throughout the land. Many flocked to her door for her 'Tree Magic' and she helped where she was able and never turned anyone away empty-handed.

When Simeon eventually died - many, many years later, it was chronicled that Fern, now a very old woman indeed, said goodbye to her children and her many grandchildren and returned back to Woolpit.

There she stayed for a short while with her old friends the Fletcher twins and then, one late summer afternoon, she left them also. It was told by one of Meg Fletcher's curly-haired grandsons, that he saw the green lady stand by the edge of Nunty's Wood and whisper a strange birdsong

up into the trees.

Moments later, a man appeared. He too was green and he wore a crown of holly upon his head; the green lady embraced him like a long-lost brother. Then, she held hands with this green king and the lad watched them pass happily into the dwindling woodlands and out of human sight forever.

Once they had gone the boy turned back to the village. Smoke from the cottages below was beginning to curl away into the sunset and then, through the trees, he heard his mother call his name. The boy smiled because he knew his supper would be on the table. And then she called him again. 'Hickory,' she cried…'Hickory!'

# Historical Note

The legendary figure of the Green Knight appears in many Arthurian tales and involves Sir Gawain, who steps forward to cut off the Green Knight's head at a Christmas feast. The strange warrior, however, replaces his head on his body and challenges Gawain to find him in a year and a day, so the Knight can return the chop.

Lyonesse is also a well-known legend and one that many believe is a British version of the Atlantis story. It centres around the history of the Isles of Scilly.

Once again the Green Man carvings can be found in churches on the map and it is interesting to note how many green men appear in churches called St Bartholomew. A coincidence, no doubt!

# Glossary

**Azure** - *the colour blue in heraldry*
**Constable** - *in charge of a castle when the Lord was away*
**Demesne** - *land belonging to the Lord*
**Device** - *design or emblem on a coat of arms*
**Godsib** - *godmother or godfather*
**Harrier** - *slender, narrow winged hawk*
**Haywain** - *cart that carried hay*
**Hayward** - *looked after the corn and hay*
**Lance** - *long wooden spear used in jousting*
**Pennant** - *flag*
**Portcullis** - *iron grill to protect the castle gateway*
**Quintain** - *a target used for practice with a lance on horseback*
**Rebec** - *medieval instrument like a violin*
**Reeve** - *official in charge of the Lord's farmland*
**Shawm** - *medieval instrument like a trumpet*
**Shieldwall** - *line of shields used in a defence wall*
**Solar** - *Lord's private room*
**Steward** - *official in charge of the Lord's manor*
**Surcoat** - *tunic with coat-of-arms upon it*
**Swineherd** - *pig farmer*
**Tithe** - *Church tax*
**Trebuchet** - *a type of catapult*
**Troubadour** - *singer of songs*
**Vassal** - *person who holds land in return for services to a lord*
**Villein** - *peasant controlled by the Lord of the manor*
**Yoke** - *wooden beam to hold the oxen*